Apartment 202

Keith Barbee

To order additional copies of this book, contact:
Xlibris Corporation
1-888-795-4274
www.Xlibris.com
Orders@Xlibris.com
57908

CONTENTS

For anyone who ever had a dream *and* pursued it . . .

1

It's Going Down

"DON'T PUT YOUR muthafuckin' finger in my face, Antonio."

"Or what, Keisha? What the fuck you gon' do?"

"Nigga, you don't scare me."

"Shut the fuck up," Antonio said with his finger still in her face.

"You gon' get yours nigga."

"Bitch, you talkin' stupid."

"Fuck you! I got yo' bitch, too. You gon' end up back at yo' mama house where I found yo' black ass."

"Who you think pay the rent?" Antonio asked. "Or did you forget?"

"But whose name is on the lease?" Keisha asked walking out of the cluttered room. Antonio watched her ass in the $300 Rock & Republic jeans he had bought her two days earlier. He moved the toothpick from the left side of his mouth to the right as Keisha disappeared into another room of the apartment they shared in southeast D.C.

"And don't walk away from me while I'm talking," he barked at her back.

Antonio grabbed the television remote and flipped the channel to his favorite show, *Jeopardy!* The 40 ounce bottle of 211 beside the black leather sofa was now warm as he sucked the piss-colored drink down in one gulp. *Jeopardy!* was about the only show he would watch besides *The Wire*, now in his overfull DVD collection.

"Who is Shakespeare," he said aloud before the contestants could answer the question 'who wrote *Romeo and Juliet?*'

Antonio grabbed a dime bag from under the seat cushion and pulled a Dutch from his Crown Holder shirt pocket. He was rolling the grape blunt when Keisha and Calandra walked in the room.

"That's exactly what's wrong with your stupid ass – smoking and drinking all the damn time," Keisha said, looking at her hair in the black-framed mirror on the wall.

"Shut up bitch. I know you see *Jeopardy!* on. Ain't nobody tryna hear that shit."

"Wassup Antonio?" Calandra said in that country North Carolina accent D.C. niggas loved.

"Oh, you speaking today wit yo' saddity ass?"

"I always speak."

"Yeah, when you tryna pull off my fuckin' blunt. Is my nigga Rell still hitting that pussy?"

"Why the fuck you in my business?"

"Because I want you to tell the nigga to holla at me when you see him again. I been calling his cell and shit but it's off or something."

"Well, I ain't seen Rell since last week and . . ."

"Bitch, I ain't asked you all that . . . Damn! You gon blow my high before I even get there."

Keisha and Calandra stood in the middle of the room and continued gossiping and talking about going shopping for shoes to wear to the club.

"You two got to get the fuck outta here with that shit. *Jeopardy!* back on from commercial."

"Call me when you get that blunt rolled," Calandra said, following Keisha out the sliding door onto the balcony.

"Girl, I thought you stopped fucking with Rell sorry ass?" Keisha asked as they stood outside.

"Keisha," Calandra looked her dead in her face. "Rell got some good dick."

"Bitch, you silly."

"I'm not lying on that nigga. He trifling as hell and I know he's fucking other chicks but that nigga lay pipe."

"Ain't no dick *that* good," Keisha said.

"Rell, ain't fucked you," Calandra said matter-of-factly.

"Whatever girl. Speaking of trifling ass niggas, I'm about to put Antonio ass out. Send him back to his mama in northwest."

Antonio walked out onto the balcony handing the burning blunt to Calandra.

"Bitch, you ain't sending me nowhere I don't wanna go," Antonio said coughing and inhaling the weed smoke simultaneously.

"Why don't you take yo stupid ass back in the apartment and watch that dumb ass show you always watching?"

"It's gone off," he said. "*You* need to be watching it. You might learn something."

Keisha rolled her eyes and looked down at the street where people were getting off from work and kids were getting off the school bus. It was mid-June and the sun was beaming down on the hood. Doug Hill had predicted a scorcher and advised children and the elderly to be especially cautious in the humid temperatures. But who listened to meteorologists anyway? D.C. definitely listened to and heeded the words of Doug Hill. During the winter months, if he said there would be snow; the supermarkets filled to capacity *immediately*. No milk. No bread. No hope.

Keisha would remind one of Robin Givens, and not just because of the $1,500 weave. She had strong facial features that were almost masculine. She had high cheekbones and a rich, alto voice. Her hands were big for a woman. She was goddess-like.

Calandra, on the other hand, was model tall and wore her hair in any number of styles. From bobbed wigs to a black afro or a short blonde style cut close like a fade, she was a trendsetter. She was a girly girl but feisty. She had one dimple on her right cheek and she definitely thought she was cute.

"You know T.I. gon be at Club Love Friday, Keisha."

"Yeah, I heard it on the radio. You tryna go?"

"Hell yeah but I ain't got shit to wear."

"You tryna go down Georgetown and find something?"

"I was really thinking Tyson's Galleria," Calandra said.

"How the fuck are we gon' get out to Virginia?"

"Antonio got several cars," Calandra said passing the blunt back to him.

"You hoes got in a wreck the last time I gave you the keys to one of my cars. The paint job alone cost me $600."

"Nigga, you hustle everyday. $600 ain't hurt you," Calandra said.

"You're right. It didn't hurt me but it didn't help me either. I could have done something else with that loot."

"Nigga, you got enough jewelry and shit. What was you gonna do with it?" Keisha asked.

"Bitch, I don't answer to you about my money."

"Anyway Antonio – can we use a car tomorrow to go out Virginia?"

"Hell nah – give you my car, put gas in it, *and* throw you some money to shop with – Are you out yo' damn mind? The two of you better sell some pussy."

"See, you talking crazy," Keisha said. "You can let us use the Lexus. You never drive it anyway."

"I don't give a fuck if I never use it again! I said no," Antonio barked, stepping back into the apartment.

"Calandra, I'll scoop you around noon tomorrow or whenever I wake up."

"Alright girl. I'm about to go. I know Lil' Tony done made it to the house by now. I'm sitting here listening to ya'll and my baby outside waiting to get in the house. I'll holla at you later," she said leaving out the front door.

2

All Falls Down

"HOW MUCH LOOT did Antonio give you? Calandra asked as they walked in Neiman Marcus.

"Antonio didn't give me shit but I took a stack out his pants pocket."

"Bitch, you gon' get fucked up," Calandra said laughing.

"Fuck Antonio!"

Keisha and Calandra breezed through Neiman's looking at designer handbags and stiletto shoes. They also paid attention to security cameras and guards as they looked at the high-end merchandise. The two twenty-something's left the store and ended up in Saks Fifth Avenue, making stops in Versace, Nicole Miller, and Chanel along the way.

"I think I'm getting that Tracy Reese blouse and that black Marc Jacobs bag from Neiman's," Calandra said putting a Chloe linen and cotton skirt on the cash wrap along with some bangles and a wide, black belt.

"That's a cute skirt," Keisha said. "What top are you wearing with it?"

"I got this cute fuschia one from Benetton down Georgetown that I haven't worn. It's a V-neck so you know the girls will be sitting up on display in it," she laughed.

"I don't know what the fuck I'm gon' do," Keisha said. "Let's stop by Burberry and Bottega Veneta before we head back to Neiman's."

Calandra paid for the items and the two stopped at Cinnabon before reaching Burberry.

"Hold up, let's stop in here right quick," Keisha said.

"Bitch, you need to hurry up. You know what we got to do and I'm not trying to be in that rush hour traffic headed home either."

"I know but I need some 'Oh Baby' and some lashes from this MAC store and we're right here at the damn place," Keisha said. "Come on."

Calandra reluctantly went in the cosmetics store with Keisha and ended up with some 'Greed' lipglass and a pair of lashes for herself.

"That color looked hot on you," Keisha said.

"I know. I had to get it girl. But come on, we gotta go ahead and do this and get the hell out of here."

Calandra sat down and waited for a salesperson to bring her the Christian Louboutin's she saw earlier in size 8 while Keisha walked around the store. Once Calandra was up in the three-way mirror admiring her southern legs and thighs in the costly stilettos, Keisha motioned for the salesperson to help her with a shoe she liked. As before, the clerk disappeared to the back, fetching a high dollar pair of shoes.

Leaving the Nine West ballet flats she wore to the store in the box, Calandra walked casually to where she had stashed the Nancy Gonzalez bag and a Rachel Roy novelty skirt for Keisha and quickly left the store. Keisha, in a pair of ridiculously priced Via Spiga's was headed toward Thomas Pink to pick Antonio up a couple pair of boxer shorts. That's all he would wear. No tighty whitey's. No briefs. No boxer briefs. Just boxers. The nigga said his shit couldn't be confined.

"If you say one more fucking thing about the traffic Calandra," Keisha said unlocking the apartment door.

"What? Then what hoe?" Calandra asked.

"What are you silly chicks arguing about now?" Antonio asked.

"Fuck you!" they both yelled.

"Fay called," Antonio said. "And you know we gotta talk Keisha."

"Talk about what nigga?" she asked.

"How my muthafuckin' money be walking up out my pockets bitch."

"Don't start that shit. We got company."

"Calandra funky ass ain't company. I need to be hollarin at her ass too cause I'm sure she helped you spend my money."

"Nigga, don't put me in that shit," Calandra said rolling her eyes. "I got my own fucking money."

"Whatever!" Antonio said. "Go on in the back somewhere with that silly shit. *Jeopardy!* will be on in a few minutes and I don't need the distractions."

"What the fuck you doing over here," Keisha asked bumping into Corey on her way to the bathroom.

"I came to re-up with Antonio," Corey said.

"Antonio, why you ain't say Corey dumb ass was over here when we walked in the door," Keisha said putting her bags down.

"Bitch, you didn't give me time with all that talking you was doing."

"How you been baby?" Keisha said kissing Corey on the cheek.

"Wassup Corey?" Calandra said flatly.

"Wassup wit' you? Where you two been?" he asked.

"Out VA shopping," Calandra said.

"Out there shopping like Paris Hilton and Nicole Ritchie I see," Corey said noticing their bags and walking back toward the front room.

Keisha and Calandra just looked at each other.

Corey was gay, but not *gay* gay. He was as masculine as any other dude in southeast which is why Rell and Antonio let him hang around. Not to mention that they all had grown up together. His complexion was akin to a rubber band, he was average height, and had a 36-inch chest from summers spent in the gym. Dusty curls sat atop his head and complimented the butterscotch of his eyes. His lips looked like they had been stung *twice* by a bumblebee. He was cute. As a matter of fact, Corey was sexy as hell but he liked the same thing Keisha and Calandra liked – dick.

He was the type of cat who knew shit dudes weren't expected to know like who Janice Dickinson was, hair dye colors like Chestnut Blonde by Dark & Lovely, and like most gay guys – he dressed his ass off. None of that makes you gay but it does make you suspect. Corey was cool as shit though. He did him in a way that didn't make people uncomfortable.

"Yo playboy, I'm about to dip," Corey said to Antonio.

"Aiiight fam, holla at yo boy," Antonio said getting up from the couch.

Calandra and Keisha were sorting out the clothes when Antonio walked in the bedroom.

"I need to holla at you," he said.

"And! Nigga, you see I'm busy," Keisha said defiantly.

"Send your lil' chickenhead friend home so we can talk Keisha."

"You done lost yo mind. I told you to stop smoking that shit everyday."

"I'm gonna go ahead and bounce Keisha. I gotta scoop Lil' Tony up from Big Mama's anyway," Calandra said grabbing her clothes off the bed and putting them back in the shopping bag.

"That's some country shit – Big Mama," Keisha laughed.

"Bye girl. Call me if Antonio gets too out of line," Calandra said eyeing Antonio and walking out the room.

"Why the fuck you always tryna embarrass me nigga?" Keisha asked once Calandra had left.

"That bitch ain't nobody!"

"Whatever! What the fuck was so important you had to come in here with that silliness?

"Ain't shit silly about me missing a couple G's."

"Don't start."

"Give me my muthafuckin' money then."

"Nigga, you not missing no fuckin' three thousand dollars. I should have taken more than that," Keisha said about to walk out the room.

"Bitch, I'm not playing," Antonio said grabbing her arm.

"See, now I know you tripping," Keisha said.

"I'm tired of you disrespecting me Keisha."

"Nigga, fuck you!"

Antonio reared back and slapped the hell out of Keisha.

"That's the shit I'm talking about – Disrepect."

Keisha stood there not believing that Antonio had actually hit her. Her eyes welled with tears she didn't know she was capable of shedding. The room circled and stopped and kept going. Keisha turned her back and walked out of the room.

3

12 Play

"WHAT YOU DOING girl?" Calandra asked Fay through the cordless telephone.

"Sitting my fat ass on this couch watching TV."

"I been thinking – a bitch need a car. I'm tired of catching Metro. You think you can take me car shopping this week?"

"We can go now if you want. I'm not doing anything. You know which dealerships you want to go to?"

"It don't matter. Just stop at the ones we pass."

"You need a better plan that that Calandra," Fay said laughing.

"Bitch, I just need a car."

"Alright, let me put some clothes on. I'll be there shortly," she said hanging up.

All 220 pounds of Fay Perkins pulled up to Calandra's apartment complex where she was already outside waiting on her cell phone.

"I understand but I have instructed Lil' Tony that if someone fucks wit him, he has permission to hit them back," Calandra said getting in Fay's dirty Ford Explorer.

"Yeah, I hear what you saying but you not really talking about shit," she said in the phone. "I'm on my way."

"Can you run me by Lil' Tony's school? He just got suspended for fighting girl," Calandra said getting off the phone.

"I'm fine and you?" Fay retorted.

"Bitch, how you doing? Can you take me by my son's school?"

"I hadn't planned on doing . . . ," Fay was interrupted.

"Girl, I got some gas money, just do me this one."

They pulled up to Tyler Elementary School. Calandra jumped out the truck and headed into the re-opened school her son attended as a third grader. Lil' Tony was sitting in the front office when his mother walked in cursing.

"Tony, who is yo' damn teacher," Calandra said to her son without acknowledging the receptionist.

"Ma'am, there are children present. Could you please refrain from profanity?" the receptionist said.

"Girl, these kids have heard these words before and worst. This is southeast D.C."

"Well, that may be true but they don't need to hear them here."

Calandra ignored the older lady who was sitting behind a raised desk.

"Tony, come on," she said walking past the front office towards the principal and vice principal offices.

"Ma'am," the receptionist hollered to Calandra's back while picking up the phone. "You are not authorized to go back there."

"Open this damn door," Calandra said knocking on Principal Dade's door.

The young, accomplished man was opening the door slowly when Calandra pushed it wide open and nearly hit him in the face.

"I need to talk to you," she said sitting down in a brown chair adjacent from the principal's desk.

"Ma'am, do you have an appointment? You can't just barge in here unannounced like this," he pleaded.

Calandra, chewing gum and straightening Lil' Tony's clothes, just looked at the principal.

"Do you hear me, ma'am?" he asked.

"Yeah, I hear you but I know it don't take no damn scheduled appointment to talk about why my son is getting suspended at the end of the school year for protecting himself. This is southeast D.C., we fight if need be."

"I understand that Ms. Spencer, but there is protocol; and both you and Tony have to follow it. If Tony was having a problem with another student, he should have alerted his teacher or someone else on staff and not taken matters in his own hands."

"Sometimes, your own hands are all you got," Calandra said defiantly. "I don't know what ya'll plan to do but Tony will be back at school tomorrow."

"Ms. Spencer, you cannot abort authority when you feel like it. That's why Tony feels as though he can do the same. The example you are showing is paltry at best."

"No sir, not this morning wit yo' big words. Talk to me like you know me," she said. "Look, I understand what you're saying and all but it don't make much sense to me that Tony would be suspended right here at the end of the year."

"We'll consider your rationale Ms. Spencer and give you a call before the end of classes today but I do think it would be wise of you to take Tony with you now. We'll see about getting him back in class tomorrow."

Calandra got up, grabbed Tony, and walked out the office as catastrophically as she had entered it.

"Girl, they crazy as hell up in there," she said to Fay once Tony was secure in the backseat.

"What happened?" Fay asked.

"Just some bullshit but Tony will be back in class in the morning. Believe that! Let's go get me a car girl."

Three hours and six car dealerships later, Calandra and Lil' Tony were parking in front of Keisha's apartment building in a white 1993 Nissan Sentra.

"Keisha, girl come downstairs," Calandra said into her wireless earpiece. "I got something I want you to see. Girl, just come downstairs. Don't nobody care that yo' hair ain't done. Ain't nobody down here anyway," Calandra said ending the call.

Keisha walked out of the building with gray booty shorts, a Hollister tank top, and a Louis Vuitton scarf tied around her head. She immediately ran over to the car.

"Bitch, let the window down. I know this not you," she said screaming past the rolled windows.

Calandra got out the car and waved her hand over the top of it in much the same way that the women on *Price is Right* did.

"Hell yeah, it's me," she said smiling, opening the doors – still in *Price is Right* model mode.

"You didn't tell a bitch you were getting a whip," Keisha said.

"Girl, it was last minute. I'm tired of taking Metro and waiting on a nigga to scoop me to take me where I need to go. A bitch had to get her own wheels."

"Well, I know how we're rolling up to Love on Friday," Keisha said getting in the car.

"I know that's right," Calandra said. "I just wanted to stop by and show you the car but I gotta get on to the house and have a long talk with this one," she said pointing at Lil' Tony. "He up at school fighting girl, bout to get kicked out right here with a week or so left of class."

"Alright girl, call me later."

Keisha walked back into the apartment and sat on the couch beside Antonio. He turned the TV off in the middle of *Jeopardy!* She looked first at the blank television screen and then immediately to Antonio.

"What's wrong with you?"

"What you mean," he asked.

"Wasn't that your favorite lil' show?" she asked glancing down at her cotton candy-colored nails.

"Look, I'm not good at this apology shit but . . ."

"It's cool Antonio," Keisha said cutting him off.

"No, it's not cool ma. I was wrong to raise my hand to you like that."

Keisha stared off into another part of the apartment.

"Baby, look at me."

With tears in her eyes, Keisha slowly turned toward the man she had fallen in love with as a teenager, the man who had gotten her pregnant at fifteen, and was there with her when she miscarried in the first trimester. Antonio grabbed Keisha by her arm and pulled her on top of him as he lay back on the couch. She first kissed him violently and haphazardly until she caught his groove.

Antonio slid his hands down her shorts where he found no trace of panties. He cupped her ass cheeks in his large hands as she grinded her hips on his massive body. Antonio pulled her shorts down below her knees and lifted her body until her pussy was right in front of his face. He could smell a hint of her freshly-shaven pubic hair. He immediately sat Keisha on his tongue. She shook gently as his tongue entered her pussy.

She became spastic as he started sucking on the fat, wet piece. He picked her up and laid her on her back on the tan carpet that ran throughout the entire apartment. Antonio opened her legs wide and found her clit. He nibbled and bit softly on it until he tasted Keisha cumming on his tongue.

Tears rolled down the side of her face until they met the carpet her back lay on. He stood up and pulled his crisp, white tee over his head and let his basketball shorts fall to the floor. Keisha got up on her hands and knees and met his dick with a wet tongue. She kissed on the head of it, tasting his precum. She licked the length of his shaft and swallowed his 9 inch dick as he played in her pussy from underneath.

Antonio sat on the floor with his back against the couch as Keisha climbed on top of him and sat down. He met her every thrust as he put her dark brown nipples in his mouth. The landline rang loud and obnoxiously. 5 minutes later, Keisha's pink Blackberry Curve began playing "Arab Money" by Busta Rhymes and Ron Browz. They acknowledged nothing but each other. Keisha laid on her back as Antonio stood up over her and bust all over her face and body. At that moment, someone knocked on the door.

"Hold the fuck up," Antonio said grabbing his yellow basketball shorts and pulling them up over his semi-erect dick.

He walked over to the door with sweat on his brow as Keisha laid in both of their cum. He partially opened the door and looked in the face of one of his regular customers.

"Hold up, dawg," he said shutting the door in the dudes face.

Keisha passed by him as he walked into the kitchen and opened the cabinet above the sink and pulled a coffee canister from behind the dried goods. He lifted the blue snap off lid and pulled a pound out and placed the can back where it was. He walked back to the door and made the exchange.

"Nigga, don't just show up at my spot again. You know better than that shit slim," Antonio said.

"Yo, I called the house phone and yo girl cell but nobody answered."

"That means we couldn't take the muthafuckin' call," Antonio said slamming the door in the dudes face again and putting the 13 Benjamin's in his sock.

Keisha was in the shower when Antonio walked to the back of the apartment. He dropped his shorts, took off his socks, and stepped into the tight shower stall with Keisha. Pressing his dick against her ass, he kissed the back of her neck and grabbed the sponge from her hands. He took the body wash and lathered the sponge and began to wash her back and arms.

He sponged her ass and thighs. Keisha arched her back when Antonio dropped the sponge, taking his hand and cupping her pussy. She moaned so inaudibly that no one heard it but the back of her teeth where the muffled sound got lost and quickly died before exiting her mouth. She turned around and kissed him full. Deep. She pulled him close to her and grabbed him by the ass as he inserted himself into her. Only the water from the shower was between them. They stood there and fucked in the shower until the water turned cold.

4

Clubbin'

"KEISHA, HURRY THE fuck up," Calandra hollered through the apartment.

"Bitch, perfection takes time."

"Well, you need to be less than perfect tonight. I aint tryna pay. You know the first 85 ladies get in free."

"Well, you could be the first one there and still not get in if being a lady is the qualifier," Keisha laughed.

"I see you got jokes. Just bring yo ass on unless you paying my way in."

"You got me fucked up. You not giving me no pussy bitch."

"You ain't never asked."

They both laughed as they grabbed their handbags and walked out of the apartment. Keisha's Betsey Johnson; Calandra's by Kate Spade.

"We gotta stop by Fay's," Keisha said as they got in the car.

"For what? I hope you ain't invite that cock-blocking bitch to the club with us."

"Nah, I didn't invite her but I just wanted to stop by to see if she wanted to roll."

"Fuck that! We already late plus I don't like that fat bitch like that anyway," Calandra said pulling onto South Capitol. "Why you hang around that big bitch anyway?"

"Fay and I grew up together. I've known her since grade school plus she's good people. She has always struggled with her weight but that never outweighed her heart and you know that," Keisha preached. "If I'm not mistaken, she's always doing shit for your ungrateful ass anyway."

"Well T.I. ain't checkin for them Mo'Nique-sized hoes tonight," Calandra said laughing.

"Fay ain't did shit to you girl," Keisha said.

"I just don't care for her. That's why I be using her simple ass. She irk me."

"Didn't she take you to get this car?" Keisha asked rhetorically. "See, that's the shit I'm talking about – ungracious."

"Didn't you hear me say I be using her ass?"

"Bust Your Window" by Jazmine Sullivan was playing on the radio.

"Girl, change the radio. I hate that damn song," Keisha said frustrated with Calandra.

Calandra hit the CD button and "Dreams" by Biggie started playing.

"I didn't know you liked B.I.G."

"Girl, that's Rell shit. I let him use the car the other day."

"Already," Keisha laughed. "Anyway, you know how Biggie talking about the industry chicks he would fuck on this song – What dudes in entertainment would you give some pussy to?

"Stringer Bell from *The Wire* is my first choice girl. Gotdamn he could get it!" Calandra exclaimed.

"Juicy J from Three 6 Mafia," Keisha added.

"Girl, Tyson Beckford is fine as hell too."

"Wendy Williams be calling dat nigga gay though."

"She call everybody gay," Calandra said. "I bet Corey know the scoop on that.

"Dwayne Wade and Jaheim can get it too."

"Remember Tank? Dat nigga can eat the pussy. You ever paid attention to his lips?"

"Girl, he sleeping with Jamie Foxx. I know you saw them on *Oprah* together," Keisha said.

"That's why I said he could eat the pussy. But you know who they say got a big dick and he always talking about sex in his lyrics?"

"Ludacris!" they both said together.

"Hell yeah girl. I heard Busta Rhymes slangin dick too."

They pulled up to the club and found a park on a side street.

"You think the car gon' be okay over here?" Calandra asked.

"It should be. There are other cars over here."

Keisha and Calandra got in line right before they cut off free entry.

"Fuckin' around with you and a bitch was about to have to pay," Calandra said sucking her teeth.

"Bitch, don't start. You already trying to fuck up my groove and we not even in the club yet."

Keri Hilson's "Turnin' Me On" was playing when Calandra's Jimmy Choo met the glassy club floor.

"This is my song," she yelled with her arms in the air. "Bitch, and the niggas in the video . . ."

"Let's post up at the bar and get some free drinks from these sucka ass dudes." "You know the lame, old cats be at the bar on this floor. We can go upstairs with them young baller niggas once we get a drink or two down here," Keisha said leading the way.

It wasn't long after the two women were standing at the bar that the bartender asked them what they would be having – compliments of a gentleman at the center of the bar. The two looked at the graying older man who politely waved in their direction. They immediately looked at each other and winked.

"Apple Martini with two cherries," Keisha stated.

"Pomegranate Martini," Calandra purred.

The two women received their cocktails and looked in the direction of the man responsible for the first of many drinks and mouthed, "thank you."

"Too easy," they said to each other and laughed.

They had made their way upstairs to the second floor and were on their third drinks, dancing to "Pop Champagne" by Ron Browz.

"Bitch, I ain't Casper. I know damn well you see me," Calandra said.

"Get the fuck out the middle of the floor then chick."

"No Bitch! Watch what the fuck you doing."

Calandra reached out and grabbed the girl in mid-sentence. "Bitch, you don't know me. I tried to be nice to yo stupid ass but I guess you can't comprehend words so maybe you'll understand this ass-whopping."

Before the altercation could get much more out of control, the club bouncers were escorting all the women out of the club separately. Calandra was cussing and fussing and still trying to get at the girl.

"It's over Calandra, damn! Let it go!"

"Fuck that. That bitch disrespected me."

"Girl, bring yo' ass on so I can at least get a half smoke and some chili cheese fries at Ben's so my *whole* night ain't fucked up."

Calandra reluctantly got in the car on the passenger side.

"Bitch, this is yo' damn car. How you gon' get in over there?"

"Keisha, just drive the damn car."

Keisha pulled the handle of the car door but it didn't open. She knocked on the window for Calandra to unlock the door. Calandra leaned over and manually rolled the window down.

"My bad bitch, that door don't open from the outside," Calandra said opening the door for her.

Keisha just shook her head and got in the car. The line was down the street at Ben's Chili Bowl so they stopped by the Carry Out joint on Southern Ave. and got chicken wings and mambo sauce.

"You know that's fucked up," Keisha said driving home.

"What the fuck you talking about?"

"We didn't even get to see T.I. because you wanna act a fool."

"Don't blame me because that bitch got out of line."

"No, bitch, you was out of line. You need to learn how to control yo' temper," Keisha said.

"Yeah, I hear you but can you pull over? I feel like I gotta throw up."

Keisha quickly pulled the car over as Calandra opened the door and hung her head out.

"And learn how to hold yo' damn liquor," Keisha said.

"Fuck you," Calandra said digging in the plastic take-out bag looking for a napkin to wipe her mouth.

5

Big Pimpin'

"WE 'BOUT TO go smoke slim," Rell said. "I know yo' broke ass didn't buy no green."

"Nah nigga, we 'bout to go smoke Jermaine shit."

"Jermaine who moe?"

"The homie uptown with the fly bitch," Rell sputtered.

"Oh that dude?" Antonio grimaced.

So you rolling with us to smoke?" Rell asked.

"I don't fuck wit too many niggas uptown yo' *especially* dat nigga Jermaine. Dat nigga foul as hell. Why you fuckin' wit' him anyway?"

"Because dat nigga have good green and he don't mind sharing."

"Yo, dat nigga just fuck wit' ya'll to see what you know going on down here. Fuck dat coward. And you need to be careful and make sure dat fool don't be lacing with something."

"Yeah, yeah, I hear you," Rell said running to catch the Metro bus.

Rell and a few other cats from southeast met up around Jermaine's spot uptown.

"Antonio thinks we need to watch out for this dude Jermaine yo. He think that nigga got ulterior motives for letting us smoke his shit," Rell said to the group of wannabe's as they walked from the bus stop a block or so to Jermaine's condo.

"Fuck that! I don't be saying shit up in his spot no way. Plus that nigga green have me tweakin for two days yo," one of the lil dudes said.

"True that," another one chimed in.

"I'm just saying. We don't need to let our guard down around this dude," Rell said.

Rell called Jermaine on his cell phone to let him know that they were downstairs. Jermaine gave him the code and buzzed them up. His condo was plush. Two 40-gallon tanks that were easily eight feet across with curving ellipses ran behind the banquettes as you walked in the door. Colorful fish crowded the water along with algae eaters, seashells, quartz gravel, coral, stingrays, jellyfish, and what looked like a baby dolphin. The living room was classy with shades of brown everywhere – beige banquettes, cherry wood end tables, chocolate picture frames with photos of his daughter and girlfriend, bookcases the color of earth, and straw baskets filled with magazines sat on the floor.

The 73 inch projection television occupied an entire wall. *Notorious*, on bootleg, was showing on it when they walked in. In the corner of the room was a bar stocked better than most clubs and on the coffee table was plastic bags filled to capacity with weed lying amongst cartons of blunts and cigarillos. That is as much of the place as Rell and his crew ever saw. It was obvious a female had decorated the place.

"What's good?" Jermaine asked.

"Ain't shit," Rell said.

"You know the drill. Help yourself to the bar and what you see on the table," Jermaine said going into the back.

Jermaine was a short dude, about 5'2 but niggas swore he was taller. It was probably the way he carried himself. He always seemed overdressed – Versace shirts, linen pants, and dress shoes. It was like the nigga was trying to prove something. Bitches loved that nigga though. Rell and the young dudes started rolling blunts and cracking his bar open when they heard a key in the door. His baby mama, Fatima, walked in with two Gucci bags, a Tiffany bag, and one from Hermes.

"Wassup Fatima?" Rell asked.

She walked into the center of the room, dropped her bags, and turned the TV off.

"Where is Jermaine," she asked in her New York accent. She was a statuesque chick from Brooklyn. She had a gold tooth on the right, lower side of her mouth. She stood there waiting on an answer as everyone stopped what they were doing and looked at her camel toe in the tight, vintage Sergio Valente jeans she had squeezed into. Even though most niggas say they don't eat pussy, most of the niggas in that room were thinking about what her pussy tasted like.

"Damn, can you niggas hear?"

"He went in the back," one of the young dudes said.

She left her bags where she dropped them and failed to cut the TV back on as she went to the back to find Jermaine. A tattoo of his name in script was at the small of her back, barely visible between the bottom of her pink baby tee and the top of her low-rise jeans. Every nigga in the hood wanted her but no nigga was man enough to step to her for fear of her man.

About two hours had passed. Neither Jermaine nor Fatima had come back into the living room area. Rell and his crew sat there and smoked a sandwich bag and a half of dude's shit and drank two bottles of Vodka, and a bottle of Hennessy. One of the young dope boys with Rell got up and started looking in Fatima's bags.

"Yo' son, get yo muthafuckin' ass out them bags before one of them comes back in here," Rell said grabbing him in his collar.

"I was just seeing what she copped."

"You was seeing what she copped and gon' fuck around and get us popped," one of the older heads said. "Sit yo' young ass back down."

Rell and his boys showed themselves out after the last blunt burned out. No one even bothered to let Jermaine know. Rell locked the door behind them as they filed out, leaving behind empty containers of cranberry juice, coke, and orange juice on the island in the kitchen and two trays full of ashes alongside empty baggies on the expensive table that sat in the middle of the well-appointed room.

6

21 Questions

"MY COUSIN SAID you need to be careful 'cause yo apartment being watched," Calandra said with no further explanation.

"Who watching my place?" Keisha laughed. "The police?"

"They always watching. I'm talking about Jermaine and his crew."

"Who he?"

"The little nigga from uptown who think he running shit," Calandra exasperated.

"Why the fuck they watching my spot?"

"Well, my cousin fucking Jermaine and she be rolling with them down to Ohio a lot. She said they got Cleveland, Akron, Cincinnati, Dayton, Elyria, Columbus, Toledo and a rack of other small cities on lock down there."

"Where the fuck yo cousin stay and shit," Keisha asked getting annoyed. "On some real shit, I don't even know that chick to trust what she saying."

"She live out Maryland. She moved up here shortly after I did. She spiteful but she wouldn't lie about that Keisha. She just got caught up with Jermaine not knowing how he rolled," Calandra continued.

"Good looking out. Tell your cousin I said thanks or whatever."

"Where Antonio, Rell, and them?" Calandra asked.

"In the streets somewhere."

"You would think they would find something better to do with their time."

"They feel like they're missing something if they not out there."

"I know. I just hope I can keep Lil' Tony out them streets. It's not like he has much in the way of a father figure. Hell, Rell still got some growing up to do."

"Girl, you just have to be mother *and* father. You have to ensure your boy becomes a man," Keisha said.

"I know but I think it's gonna be hard competing with the lures of the street. There's something about that fast life that seems to attract our men."

"I agree so what can we do when the allure is so overwhelming to them?" Calandra asked.

"That's a question they should put on that damn game show Antonio is always watching."

"It's hard out here for a single mother, Keisha."

"I know but you are the strongest bitch I know Calandra. You have to be a rock for Lil' Tony."

"And whose gonna be a rock for Calandra?"

"Don't get soft on me now Thelma."

"I can't help it Louise. Sometimes a bitch just needs a break."

"I know girl," Keisha said. "You and Lil' Tony are going to be fine as long as you keep believing."

"But what happens if my prayers, hopes, and dreams for my child just aren't enough?"

"Then they just aren't but you can't get hung up on that as long as you know that you did all that you could with all that you had."

7

Put It On Me

"CUBA GOODING, JR. got a nice ass." Keisha said getting up from the couch.

"Keisha, I don't give a fuck about that man's ass," Antonio snarled, having just watched the DVD of *Shadowboxer*.

"And you better not!" she said.

"I'm not that nigga Rell."

"What does that mean?"

"I know you've heard them hood rumors," Antonio said following behind her. "Hell, one of your girls probably started it."

"What rumors nigga?"

"That Rell and Corey fucking around?"

Keisha laughed.

"That ain't no damn rumor. Rell fucking around with both Corey and the lil' dude with Napoleon complex from uptown from what I hear."

"Stop lying on my boy! That's just hate. I only fuck with him about it because it's funny but I know Rell ain't gay."

"Whatever Antonio. You need to watch yo' boy. He got tendencies with his fake straight ass."

"How do you know Keisha?"

"Because Fay said they were at her house playing XBOX one day and she walked in the back room and saw Corey sucking Rell's dick."

"That don't mean he's gay because he let a nigga suck his dick."

"Well it definitely don't mean he's straight either."

"Girl, you bugging," Antonio said. "The nigga with the dick in his mouth is the faggot."

"Yeah, whatever. You just watch that nigga."

"Anyway, did you like the movie?"

"Hell yeah! Did you not see Cuba's ass?" she said again. "They showed it like eight times."

"Bitch, I told you that dude ass don't interest me!"

"I just wanted to be sure," she said. "The movie was good. Mo'Nique did her thing. What did you think?"

"It was cool. I liked Mo'Nique and Macy Gray was off the hook."

"Yeah, their parts could have been bigger though," Keisha observed. "You know how Cuba and that white chick had sex in the woods?"

"Yeah," Antonio said. "What about it?"

"We should do some shit like that."

Antonio was silent, pensive even.

"Go throw on something right quick," he quipped.

"For what nigga?" Keisha asked. "I'm about to wash dishes."

"Just do what I asked you girl. Damn!"

Keisha stopped running the dish water and went in the back. Twenty minutes later, they were in the Expedition headed to a destination unknown by Keisha.

Antonio drove the big, black truck at a much faster speed than what was posted, listening to Jadakiss. He pulled up at a small parking lot in one part of Rock Creek Park.

"Why you stopping here," Keisha asked.

Antonio unzipped his shorts and pulled his dick out of the slit in his boxers. Keisha looked out the tinted windows and saw no one. She pulled her hair behind her ear and began sucking Antonio's dick. His thrusts met her bobbing. She immediately put the entire dick in her mouth. Antonio fucked her throat.

"Suck that dick," he said with her hair in his hand.

Keisha gagged as she took the length of his dick up to his balls in her mouth. Antonio saw a man walk in front of the truck with his dog yelping beside him. He never bothered to alert Keisha of the closeness of company. Keisha climbed over the front seat and let the middle row of seats down. She was taking her Capri's off and had unbuttoned her blouse when Antonio got out of the truck and re-entered from the back driver's side. He looked around the perimeter of the park and closed the door of the massive truck. He kneeled in between Keisha's legs and licked her pussy *once*. She shook.

Antonio dropped his already unzipped shorts and white boxers. His dick slid right in Keisha as if her pussy had been expecting him. She grabbed his waist and guided him inside. She closed her eyes. He looked out the dark windows. Keisha slid off his dick and got on all fours. Her pussy hung low in anticipation. Antonio quickly fed it. Keisha's face was pressed against the window as she tried to find something to grab and hold on to.

Antonio climaxed and left his semen inside Keisha. She was buttoning her blouse, back in the front passenger seat. The clock on the dash read 4:15 p.m.

8

Silly Ho

THERE WAS A knock on the door.

"Let me in this bitch!"

Knocking – harder. Louder. With more intensity. Calandra basically fell through the door when Keisha opened it.

"Where that fuckin' faggot at?"

"Calm down girl? Who you talking about?"

"Corey. I know his bitch ass over here. His muthafuckin' cousin said he was with Antonio," Calandra shouted looking over Keisha's shoulder.

"Girl, what the hell is wrong with you coming over here at 2:00 in the morning, knocking on my door like you misplaced yo' good sense?" Keisha asked pulling Calandra inside the dark apartment.

"I know he's in here. You can stop hiding his bitch ass."

"Corey is not over here."

"Well, where the fuck he at?"

"I don't know. I'm one of the few people who obviously ain't fuckin' wit' the nigga so you need to ask somebody who getting the dick *or ass*. And it seems like that list is only getting longer so you got a lot of people you can ask. But, one of them ain't me."

"Keisha, I'm not fuckin' playing. I'm beating his ass when I see him."

"For what?" Keisha asked sitting down on the couch and turning on a lamp.

"For fucking around with Rell."

"Where did you hear that Calandra?"

"Bitch, don't play. Word is I'm the last somebody to know."

"Well, the people who it affects usually are."

"So you know?"

"I didn't say that," Keisha countered. "Know what *exactly?*"

A key turned in the lock. Keisha and Calandra both looked up. Antonio walked into the apartment. Corey was behind him.

"There that bitch-made nigga is!" Calandra jumped up, lunging at Corey.

"Yo Keisha, control your girl," Antonio said stepping in between Calandra and Corey.

"Fuck that. Let that 'ho go. I'll fuck her country ass up," Corey said.

"Shut up sissy," Calandra said reaching for Corey.

"Yo Antonio, let her go," Corey said.

Calandra broke past Antonio and grabbed Corey's shirt, ripping it. In her nightgown, Keisha ran toward Calandra while Antonio grabbed Corey. Calandra managed to slap the shit out of Corey before Keisha tackled her to the floor.

"Hell nah, I'm fucking you up bitch," Corey shouted.

"Yo, what the fuck is going on?" Antonio demanded.

"That pussy ass nigga you hanging with sucking my nigga dick," Calandra offered.

"Don't you need to take that up with yo' nigga?" Antonio asked. "Besides, who ain't sucking Rell's dick?"

"Oh, it's like that Antonio?" Calandra asked.

"Hell yeah. You all in my apartment and shit acting a fucking fool. Yeah, it's like that," Antonio said.

"Aiiight muthafucker, we'll see," Calandra said. "Keisha, watch yo' nigga. He seem to know a lot about who sucking whose dick," Calandra said leaving out the door.

"Corey, come on back here to the bathroom so I can put some alcohol on those scratches," Keisha said.

Antonio fell to the couch. Corey followed Keisha.

"Look, I don't know what the fuck is going on with you and Rell but the streets is talking," Keisha said pulling the bottle of rubbing alcohol from the cabinet under the sink.

"Ain't shit going on," Corey said.

"Nigga, don't lie," Keisha said. "All I'm saying is fall back with that shit until the buzz die down."

"I hear you."

"Nigga, you better act like it before shit gets out of hand," Keisha said. "Calandra is a crazy bitch. And I say that with all the love I have."

"Dat nigga Rell packing like shit though," Corey said.

"Yeah, I've heard," Keisha said laughing. "I know you've heard big dicks ain't nothing but trouble."

"Some trouble is worth it though," he said.

Keisha and Corey walked back to the front of the apartment where Antonio had fallen asleep.

"Aye dawg," Corey said nudging Antonio. "I'll catch up with you tomorrow."

"It's already tomorrow," Antonio said rising up and stretching.

"Well, later today," Corey said.

"Aiiight money," Antonio said giving Corey pound, closing the door behind him and locking it.

"These muthafuckers wildin' around here," Antonio said to Keisha.

"You ain't never lied baby but that's what happens in the summer. Niggas loose they minds. Come on and get in the bed," she said pulling him by his tatted arm.

9

Can't Deny It

LIL' TONY ENDED the school year with his friends. Of course, he went back the day after his mama acted a fool in the front office. Most of the school's personnel thought Calandra was capable of anything and therefore felt compelled to let the boy back in class despite his persistent disruptive behavior.

On the last day of school, Calandra picked him up early because he was taking the bus to North Carolina to spend the summer with his grandparents.

Calandra grew up in a middle-class neighborhood with a two car garage, manicured lawn, and above-ground pool. She was spoiled. Her older brother had gotten killed in a motorcycle accident when she was in junior high school. They were extremely close. Her parents even had to put her in therapy because she couldn't deal with the loss.

She began acting out. Calandra was fly out the womb and quickly grew into her southern fried body. A body that defied her young age. She was promiscuous and defiant. She thought she wanted sex but she was longing for attention; for love. She found the attention in places she shouldn't have. The love, she was still seeking.

"You sure Tony and Jeremy gon' be okay on that bus by themselves girl," Keisha asked en route to the Greyhound station.

"Jeremy is 16. He knows what to do and what not to do. Plus, Lil' Tony looks up to his ugly ass," Calandra said looking in the back seat at the two cousins.

"I know but girl that's like a nine hour bus trip, ain't it?"

"Something like that – Nine or 10 hours. They'll be alright though, Jeremy got his lil cell phone and whatnot."

Jeremy grabbed both his bag and Lil' Tony's from the trunk of the car and started walking toward the terminal.

"Boy, if you don't get over here and give me a damn hug," Calandra said.

Jeremy circled back and dropped the bags to give Calandra a hug. She then grabbed and hugged her son tight as she kissed him on the cheek.

"You gon' be good this summer?" she asked the seven year old boy.

"I might," he joked.

"You *might?*" Calandra asked. "Well, don't call me when Granny beat that butt."

"He'll be cool," Jeremy said. "I'll have him hanging with me most of the time."

"And that's the damn problem," Calandra said pushing Jeremy in his head.

"Seriously, he good," Jeremy said.

"I know. Ya'll be good down there and enjoy yourselves. I'll probably run down there 4th of July if I can get Keisha to roll with me."

Keisha rolled her eyes in disgust at the thought of spending the holiday in hot ass North Carolina with nothing to do. Calandra watched as the two boys walked into the station.

"Is Lil' Tony's daddy in North Carolina, too," Keisha asked on the ride back home.

"Don't be asking me no questions about his daddy. I don't even wanna *think* about that nigga let alone *talk* about him."

"Obviously bitch because I don't even know shit about the nigga and I'm supposed to be your best friend. The *only* fuckin' thing I can even come up with is that the nigga's name is Tony. And the only Tony that I know *you* know lives with me," Keisha joked.

"Well, ain't much to say about him except we met, we fucked, and Lil' Tony appeared nine months later," Calandra said. "But there is a nigga who I do wanna talk about."

"Who bitch? Details . . ."

"Should I let Rell move in?"

"Heffa, I thought you was about to drop some good gossip," Keisha said flatly. "And yo' ignorant ass thinking about moving Rell wanna-be rapper ass in."

"Well, we have been messing around for a while now."

"And that means he has to move in?" Keisha asked. "Take it from a bitch who is living with a nigga like Rell now. That shit ain't always what it seems."

"I mean, he do help you with bills and shit though."

"Yeah but muthafuckers be watching my spot, too."

"I guess that comes with the territory."

"I guess so," Keisha agreed. "You really serious about Rell moving in aren't you?"

Calandra was quiet.

"Bitch, you hear me."

"I mean, why not? He's always over there anyway."

"I hope you've thought this through," Keisha said.

"I have."

"So you know what you doing?"

"Not really but we'll figure it out as we go," Calandra said.

"And how does Lil' Tony feel about this move-in father?"

"Lil' Tony don't get no vote."

"He should."

"He don't pay no bills."

"But he's affected," Keisha said.

"I see you tryna complicate shit."

"Not anymore than it already is. I'm just saying, don't be moving niggas in and out your space and your son's life just because the dick is good."

"It's not just about the dick," Calandra said.

"I hope not."

10

Wet Wipes

COREY WALKED IN Malcolm X Park for the first time wearing gray sweats, fresh Dunks, an Ed Hardy shirt, a Washington Nationals fitted and no underwear. The park was a known gay cruise spot. Corey had heard about it from a few cats he ran with but never considered going. He pulled the navy blue cap down low over his eyes and walked with his head down.

He passed a fat guy or two, some feminine dudes, and several old cats. He was about to head out the park when he saw a yungin he had scoped on the Metro train a few times. The two had made eye contact and kept it moving on the train but tonight they stopped, stared, and fidgeted.

"Sup fam?" Corey said.

The athletic-built guy nodded his head as he looked at Corey and then away into the distance. Corey walked past him and down the stairs. The guy met him on the other side of the park.

"So wassup," he asked.

"You tell me yung."

"I'm tryna bust this nut playboy," the wheat-colored boy said.

"That's wassup," Corey said with his hand in his sweats.

"You know a spot to go to?" the guy asked.

"Nah yo, it's my first time out this joint."

"Follow me."

Corey and his new-found friend of 5'8, 144 pounds, walked to the far end of the park with little conversation. They came to a clearing and ducked under several tall trees. Both dudes just stood there. Two other dudes walked by and quickly ducked into a bush close to them.

"It's hot out here tonight," the guy offered. "Niggas is everywhere."

He pulled Corey's dick out from the heat of the sweatpants and bent over. Corey closed his eyes as the wetness of homeboy's tongue met the heat of his dick.

"Yo son, you gottta look out," the dude said seeing that Corey had his eyes closed. "5-0 be running up in here after hours."

Corey quickly opened his eyes and started scouting the park.

"What's yo' name yo," Corey asked the guy.

"This *is* yo' first time," the guy took Corey's dick out his mouth long enough to say.

"Hold up, here come somebody," Corey said as another guy approached to watch.

The dude sucking his dick stood up and played coy.

"What nigga?" Corey asked the dude standing there tryna watch them freak. "Get the fuck on yo before I fuck you up."

The dude walked away as Corey's freak partner pulled his dick out.

"Damn son, it's like that," Corey said admiring the dude's 10 inch dick.

The two stood there and jacked off until nut left both their dicks and fell to the ground. The dude walked off without even a head nod. Corey stood there wondering how he was gon get the nut off his hand.

11

It's Not Right But It's Okay

RELL, ANTONIO, AND Corey were standing on the corner waiting for something to happen as was typical for them. Rell, in usual fashion, started spitting.

In D.C. like the Nationals/ a nigga be international
From Asia to Africa/ the rhymes be spectacular
Still holding down the block/ Keep my girl full of cock
Jay ain't the only nigga wit spit/ Ask my girl who makes it fit
In the tightest of places/ Fuckin' wit chicks wit MAC on they faces
Slim rocking True Religions/ Got these hoes losing they religion
And calling on a higher cause/ I'm hot just because
Just matter-of-fact/ She hooked from the sex act
And the verbal skills/ Uma ain't the only one who killed Bill
From dollars to making sense/ I ghostwrite for 50 Cent
And show up on yo myspace page/ Fuck that! The world is my stage

"Yeah, yeah, yeah nigga," Antonio teased.
"That was hot son," Corey said.

"I appreciate that my dude," Rell said to Corey. "This nigga Antonio hatin' and shit."

"Nigga, ain't nobody hatin' on yo simple ass."

"Yeah, whatever," Rell said.

Rell went into another freestyle while they stood out on the corner of Chesapeake and Barnaby and blazed.

"One of ya'll need to let me hold something 'til the first," Tootsie said walking up on the group.

"*Need*," Antonio exclaimed. "Get yo crackhead ass out of here. You know damn well ain't no credit in the streets."

"I'll eat yo ass," she said walking away.

"Ain't that some shit?" Rell said laughing. "I remember when they used to just offer to suck yo' dick. Damn, times done changed."

"Yo for real, Tootsie Pop used to be the shit out here. How you think she got that name?" Corey asked.

"Nigga, I didn't even know it was Tootsie Pop. All I ever known was Toot," Antonio said.

"Quick history lesson then homeboy. I don't know her real name or no shit but I do know that she was a dime at one time and got turned out yo. The nickname came about because niggas said she looked so good, they would eat the middle and you know niggas ain't too quick to *publicly* say they'll eat some pussy," Corey said.

"How the fuck you know all this nigga?" Antonio asked.

"Fay be talking about that shit at the house."

"Well shorty ain't no dime now," Antonio said.

"Shorty eating ass," Rell laughed.

"The ambulance just carried Fay off to the hospital," Missy said out of breath.

"Whoa, back up Missy and slow the fuck down," Corey said.

"It's Fay!"

"What about her?"

"The ambulance just took her," Missy screamed.

"Come on nigga, I'll take you to see what's going on," Antonio offered.

"I don't even know where the fuck they took her," Corey rationalized.

"Since DC General closed, there ain't too many places they gonna take no nigga but Howard," Rell said.

"Damn straight," Antonio said gunning the silver Mustang that he rarely drove.

Keisha and Calandra were already there in the waiting room when they arrived.

"Yo what happened?" Corey asked. "Have they said anything?"

"Calm down first," Keisha instructed taking Corey by his hand and sitting him down.

"Baby, go get him some water," she said to Antonio.

Calandra and Rell sat down across from them.

"Is she alright?" Corey asked again.

"She will be," Keisha assured. "She had a miscarriage."

"Miscarriage?" Corey asked. "I didn't even know she was pregnant."

"Well, from what we know, she didn't either," Keisha said.

Antonio handed Corey a bottle of water as a doctor walked up to the group of friends.

"How is she?" Corey asked.

"She's resting but she'll be fine. Because of the stress of her weight, Ms. Perkins was unable to carry the child to term unfortunately," the physician said. "And due to the weight, she also didn't even know that she was pregnant."

"Can we see her," Keisha asked.

"One or two of you at a time should be okay but you don't want to overwhelm her," he said. "I'll take two of you now if you like."

Keisha and Corey walked behind the doctor.

"Wait here," he said.

The doctor ducked inside Fay's room to see if she felt like company. He came back to the door.

"Go on in, she wants to see you."

Fay looked 10 pounds lighter in the hospital bed. Her skin was pekid but she was smiling. Corey walked slowly up to the side of the bed.

"Nigga, I know you not acting scared up in here," Fay said.

"I just didn't know . . ." Corey said trailing off.

"It's okay nigga. A bitch just too big. I ain't seen you this upset since Grandma Carolyn passed."

"I know," Corey managed. "You called Auntie?"

"And tell her what?" Fay asked. "That I lost a baby I was carrying out of wedlock. You know damn well how my mother and her religion are. She's almost as bad as your mama when it comes to her Jesus. They ain't sisters for nothing."

"True," Corey said.

Corey had moved in with Fay and his Aunt Norma Jean and her second husband, Bob when he was an experimenting teenager. His own parents couldn't separate themselves from their religion, their morals, and their values long enough to love Corey like he felt he needed. He ran away from home constantly. His parents finally made arrangements for him to live with his aunt and uncle so that they at least knew where he was and that he was safe.

He and Fay grew up like sister and brother.

"How did you all find out I was here?"

"Missy came down on the block all out of breath," Corey said.

"Missy from next door?" Fay asked rhetorically. "That's a nosey bitch."

"It was a good thing she was nosey this time or we wouldn't have known that the ambulance had come to the house. We just guessed that they brought you here."

"You know this is where they bring us to die," Fay laughed.

"Don't be saying that," Keisha said walking up to Fay and kissing her on the cheek. Fay grabbed her hand.

"How you doing, ma?" Keisha asked.

"I've been better," Fay said. "But I'll be okay girl."

"You know you gotta loose some weight, don't you?" Keisha asked solemnly.

Fay shook her head yes. A tear rolled down her plump face.

"We love you girl. And we will *not* loose you because of your weight," Keisha said.

And almost on cue; Calandra, Rell, and Antonio walked through the door.

"You all are not supposed to be in here," Keisha said.

"Fuck they rules," Rell said.

"Ain't nobody thinking about these damn doctors," Antonio added.

"Our homegirl in here. Why can't we be in here with her? Calandra stated.

Everybody looked at each other and started laughing as they each went up to Fay and let her know how they felt about her and how much she scared them. The doctor walked back in the room and let them know that they would have to leave so that Fay could rest. They collectively said goodbye and left the room, escorted by the doctor. Corey loitered a bit longer in the room with Fay.

"You know I love yo fat ass," he said.

"I know sissy," Fay responded.

They laughed and hugged.

"See you when you get home," Corey said.

12

You Already Know

A NTONIO PULLED UP in front of Calandra's apartment building and blew the horn of his white Chrysler 300. The rims kept spinning as he waited for Rell to come downstairs.

"Sup slim?" Rell said opening the car door.

"Wassup wit' you?" Antonio asked.

"Glad to get out the house yo."

"Damn nigga, you just moved in and you already getting in yo' feelings?" Antonio teased.

"It is what it is. You know how chicks can be."

"No doubt," Antonio said. "I gotta run out to the H.O.B.O. shop and cop some shit before we make this run. Dat cool?"

"Hell yeah yo. I ain't been in that joint in a minute. Shit cost just as much as Sean John and that other shit."

"I know yo but it's good shit. You know what I'm sayin? Good quality plus it's local so a nigga gotta support it."

"No doubt," Rell said. "Oh yeah, the boy Corey called and said scoop him, too."

Antonio pulled up to Fay and Corey's house which their grandmother willed to them. Antonio blew the horn but Corey never came out.

"Yo, go get that fool," Antonio said, putting the car in park.

Rell knocked on the door and then just walked on in the house when he realized the front door was unlocked. Rell walked slowly through the row house until he heard faint noises. He peeked through an ajar bedroom door and saw Corey bent over in a pair of Timbs getting fucked by some big muscle dude. He bust the door open and stood there as Corey arched his back and took the dick like a bitch. The dude stopped. Corey looked up. Rell walked out the room.

"He should be out in a minute," Rell said getting back in the car.

"Yo, what the fuck he doing?" Antonio asked. "We gotta go."

"Getting fucked," Rell said obviously pissed.

"What nigga?" Antonio asked surprised but laughing.

"You heard me. That nigga getting his back beat the fuck out."

The muscle dude walked out of the front door.

"Yo, I seen that nigga somewhere before," Antonio said. "That kid was fucking our lil homie?"

"Yeah," Rell said, nonchalantly.

"Damn!" Antonio laughed and blew the horn again. "So you mad nigga?"

Rell was quiet.

"I'm gon' leave that shit alone. You niggas wild as hell," Antonio smirked.

Corey walked out the house with his jeans unzipped, pulling an LRG t-shirt over his head.

"You could have told us you had plans nigga," Antonio said. "We could have made moves without you."

"It's cool. I guess it's official now, huh?" Corey said. "No more speculating."

"I guess so yung," Antonio said.

"I didn't really wanna believe that shit but do you fam."

Rell was quiet the entire drive to the H.O.B.O shop. Antonio was trying on some shit in the back while Rell and Corey walked around the store.

"You mad yo?" Corey asked.

"Nigga, Fuck you!" Rell said.

"Whatever yo. You knew what it was."

"I guess it's true what they be saying about you homo niggas," Rell snided.

"And what's that Rell?"

"It's all about the sex and ya'll fuck anything moving."

"Nigga, like I said – you knew what it was."

Antonio came from the dressing room with a handful of shit that he threw up on the cash wrap.

"Ya'll see anything ya'll want?" he asked. "Grab it and throw it up here before I change my mind."

Corey and Rell both reached for the same hoodie.

"I got it yo," Corey said.

"Nah, I got it homeboy," Rell said.

"I think we got a few more in the back," the salesclerk offered. "I'll go check."

"Ya'll fools acting real girly right about now," Antonio said.

The bronze-hued salesclerk brought Corey back the same hoodie that Rell had but in another color.

"I thought blue would look good on you," she flirted.

"Oh word, ma?"

"Yeah, I'm gon need to see for myself though so take my number so I can get a good look at you rockin it."

"You do better to give my rottweiler the number," Rell mumbled. "Dude ain't gon use it."

"You ain't got no damn rottweiler," Antonio said.

"Exactly."

Antonio burst out laughing as he signed the credit card receipt. He stopped at the corner they usually post up at. Rims still spinning.

"Get out!"

"Yo, I thought we was going with you to handle some business?" Rell asked.

"Nah homie. Not today. Ya'll niggas too vulnerable to handle business with me today. It's like ya'll having some kind of lover's quarrel and I can't work with all that tension and shit," Antonio said.

Rell opened the car door and got out with his H.O.B.O. bag.

"Yo, drop me back at the house," Corey said from the backseat.

"Nigga, get yo muthafuckin' ass out my car."

Antonio drove off. Corey ad Rell stood in the middle of the street dumbfounded.

13

Soon As I Get Home

"DID LIL' TONY and Jeremy make it to North Carolina okay?"

"Hell yeah and Lil' Tony been calling worrying the hell out of me every since they got there."

"About what?" Keisha asked.

"Talking about he bored and ain't got nothing to do."

"I thought he was gon' be hanging with Jeremy?"

"You know Jeremy man-child ass wasn't gon' wanna be taking Tony young ass with him everywhere," Calandra said.

"Speaking of something to do, we need to do something this weekend since Fay out the hospital. You know, get her spirits up and shit," Keisha said walking around the BLVD at the Capital Centre.

"True," Calandra said. "What you thinking?"

"Let's go to Zanzibar. I ain't been there in a minute."

"What night is that?"

"Saturday night is the good night," Keisha answered.

"Cool with me."

"Ladies Night."

"Yeah, that's wassup," Calandra said half-assed.

"Well, we gotta get some shit to wear since we out."

"Bitch, I ain't tryna get shit out here and see 20 hoes rockin it in the club. Are you crazy?"

"Well we can go somewhere else tomorrow but I gotta get back to the house. I told Antonio I would be there when he got back from New York."

"What he go up there for?"

"Girl, what else?" Keisha said.

"That's right. Rell was supposed to go but he said he changed his mind and wanted to stay at home with me."

"Really now?" Keisha said laughing.

"Bitch, why you laughing? I think that's sweet."

"It is. You driving to the club this weekend right?" Keisha asked changing the subject.

"My car gotta go in the shop plus Fay can't fit her big . . ."

"So that's a no?" Keisha said getting pissed.

"My bad girl. It just slipped out."

"I'm sure," Keisha said. "I'll get one of Antonio's cars."

"Aiiight girl. Call me," Calandra said slamming the door to the Expedition once they pulled up to her building.

Antonio was already in the apartment when Keisha walked in.

"Damn baby, I was tryna be here when you got in," she said.

"It's cool baby girl," he said patting her ass. "I'm just glad to see you."

Keisha put her arms around her man's neck and kissed him.

"I'm glad to see you, too."

"Where you coming from?"

"Me and Calandra went out to The BLVD."

"Spending money," he said.

"Not really. We just didn't have shit to do plus I wanted some ice cream from Cold Stone and some Chick-fil-A."

"Damn, you bring me some?"

"You know I did but it's probably all melted now."

"It'll re-freeze. Good looking baby."

"No doubt. How was your trip?"

"Long. I got business handled though and that's all that really matters but now I'm tryna handle business with you."

"I'm on my period," Keisha said.

"Baby, stop lying. Yo' period come at the end of the month and it's the fuckin' 15th."

"It's early," she teased.

"Oh, so you was giving my pussy away while I was gone? That's why you don't wanna give me none?" Antonio teased. "'Cause I'll damn sure know. That kitty fit 'Tonio dick and I could tell if it were ever tampered with."

"Maybe."

"*Maybe?*" Antonio retorted.

"I'm just fucking with you baby."

"You better be," he said. "So wassup? Can a nigga get some?"

"You gotta do something to prove how much you want it."

"Do what?"

"Go to CVS and get me a douche," she laughed.

"A *douche?* You trippin yo."

Keisha pulled her American Apparel tank over her head revealing her hard brown nipples. Gyrating her hips, she licked her middle and index fingers and put them down her Juicy Couture sweatpants. She took the fingers out of her pussy and put them in Antonio's mouth. By the time she removed her fingers, he had grabbed his keys and wallet.

"I'll be right back," he said as the door slammed behind him. "I'm on a douche run."

14

Gangsta Lovin'

"WHAT WAS THAT shit about the other day?" Rell asked passing the ball to Corey.

"What shit?"

"Real talk nigga . . . don't play with me."

"You saw what was up Rell."

"Who was that nigga?"

"Fuck if I know. I met him on the Metro. Well, I met him at the park but I had seen him on the train."

"What muthafuckin' park." Rell asked shooting the ball.

"The park over on like 15th and W Streets NW."

"What was you doing up there?"

"I was just up there."

"Yo whatever nigga. You better watch yo'self."

"Nah nigga, you better watch yo' girl 'cause the next time that bitch step to me about you . . ."

"Don't even go there with that. You know how she is."

"Yeah, I know. I know, I'm gon fuck her silly ass up the next time," Corey said hitting the backboard.

Rell sank the last basket.

"Game!"

"You wanna play another," Corey asked.

"Nah, I'm good. That was my third time beating you. You should be tired of ass-whoppings for one day."

"I hear you," Corey said grabbing his jersey and a bottle of Vitamin Water from the bench.

"What you about to do?" Rell asked.

"Go home."

"Fay there?"

"Nah, she gon' shopping with yo girl and Keisha."

"You mind if a nigga come through and take a shower?"

"That's cool," Corey said.

Corey and Rell walked the few blocks from the park back to Corey's.

"The towels are in the closet by the sink," Corey said showing Rell to the shower.

"Cool."

Corey walked out the bathroom as Rell dropped his Nike basketball shorts. Rell turned the water on in the shower and waited for it to get hot. Corey went in his room and checked the messages on his cell phone. There was one. It was from the dude who he had now been with twice whose name he still didn't know.

"You alright in there?" Corey asked opening the bathroom door.

"I'm good yo but you could come and wash my back," Rell replied.

Corey took off his green Celtics shorts and basketball jersey. He opened the shower door and stepped in. The hot water immediately found his face. And soon after, so did Rell. He looked Corey dead in his eyes and watched the water roll down his face. He moved in closer to him and allowed his lips to find Corey's. Water entered their mouths as their tongues wrestled. Rell turned his back to Corey and handed him a sponge and body wash.

Corey lathered the sponge and began to wash Rell's back. The water splashed against his skin and washed the soap down the drain. Corey paid attention to lather under Rell's arms, the back of his neck, the small of his back, and the crack of his ass. He leaned up against Rell's back and kissed his neck as the water attempted to separate them. Rell turned the water off. It trinkled. He turned around and started sucking on Corey's nipples. Lowering himself, he put Corey's dick in his mouth. Corey moaned. Precum was on Rell's tongue when he put it back in Corey's mouth.

"Do I get what you gave that other nigga?" Rell whispered in Corey's ear.

"Is that what this is about?"

"Nah, I'm just saying though."

"You can get whatever you want," Corey said. "You know that."

They stepped out the shower and walked to Corey's room where they fell on the bed. Corey opened the nightstand and grabbed two Magnums and a bottle of Platinum WET. He helped Rell put the condom on and lubed it as well as his hole. He positioned himself in the middle of the bed and allowed Rell to enter him slowly for the first time. Corey bit into the pillow as Rell fucked him for not letting him fuck him sooner. It was fast and furious. He pulled out and quickly removed the condom, shooting nut all on Corey's back and the bed sheets.

They both lay on their backs in the wet bed of sweat, shower water, and semen.

15

Freak Like Me

"COME THROUGH," JERMAINE typed into his iPhone.

"Bet," was the response.

Marcus pulled up to Jermaine's in a silver Range Rover. His athletic body and hazel eyes defied convention. Wearing an Armani suit and Prada loafers, he let himself in the condo Jermaine shared with Fatima. Because they didn't want to be burdened with child-rearing; Fatima and Jermaine's daughter lived in Brooklyn with her parents.

"What's good boy?" Jermaine asked.

"You know how I do," Marcus responded pouring himself a glass of Maker's Mark and Ginger Ale at the bar.

"What's the word out there on the street?"

"Ain't too much popping except that nigga Antonio still in yo' pockets. You know he got southeast locked down and the word is he moving into northeast."

"I see," Jermaine said finding an episode of BET's *American Gangster* he had on DVR.

"You ever watch this shit?"

"I caught a few episodes," Marcus said.

"You should watch it. You could learn from it," he said.

Fatima walked through the living room wearing only a zebra-print, lace bra and panty set. She didn't even speak to Marcus; didn't look at him.

"You want some breakfast baby?" she asked Jermaine.

"A cup of coffee is good."

Marcus removed his suit coat as Fatima disappeared into the kitchen.

"You know I fuck with a lot of chicks," Jermaine stated.

"Yeah . . ." Marcus said.

" . . . But Fatima got the best pussy I ever had. It's sweet like honeydew and fat as a kitten," he laughed. "Plus she be doing tricks and shit. I never seen nothing like it."

Marcus sipped on his bourbon and watched the rest of the *American Gamgster* episode.

"You know we gotta deal with these niggas soon," Jermaine said as Fatima brought a cup of coffee to him with a few sugar packets and a couple creamers.

"Yeah, I know," Marcus said. "I'm working it all out now yo."

"Yo' plan better be sound nigga. No loose ends."

"It's broken down in phases yo. I got a few attention-getters before we bring out the real heat."

"I like that," Jermaine said. "My nigga!"

Marcus finished his drink, grabbed his jacket, and left. Fatima walked back into the living room with whipped cream on her pussy and a cherry in her mouth.

"I decided you needed to eat something for breakfast anyway," she said straddling his face.

16

Girlfight

"I DON'T WANT no shit from you tonight," Keisha said.
"I can't promise you nothing," Calandra said.

"Whatever bitch. I hope Fay ass ready."

"She just ought to be. It ain't like she got a closet full of fly shit to choose from."

"See, that's the shit I'm talking about," Keisha said.

"Well . . ."

"Anyway, you know we going to the Go-Go instead of Fur?"

"No, I didn't know," Calandra said. "Who damn idea was that?"

"Fay's. It's her night and that's where she wanted to go."

"Figures," Calandra deadpanned. "But that means we have to drive all the way out Waldorf some damn where. That's where most the good ones be at, I hear."

"I guess we headed to Charles County then, huh?"

Keisha pulled the Expedition in front of Fay's house which was across from Nationals Park.

"It's time to party bitch," Keisha yelled knocking on the door.

Calandra popped her gum and swatted at a mosquito swirling around the porch light. Fay came to the door in a t-shirt and biking shorts.

"No ma'am," Keisha said looking disgusted. "I know you not going out looking like that?"

"I'm not going," Fay said.

"Cool. Come on Keisha, we can still get in Fur free if we hurry up," Calandra said.

Keisha shot Calandra the evil eye.

"Girl, this is supposed to be your night," she said to Fay.

"I'm just not up to it." Fay said allowing the two women in the house.

Taking Fay by the hand, Keisha led her upstairs to the closet and picked out a purple V-neck blouse and some black jeans for Fay to wear.

"You already showered, I hope," Calandra said.

"Yeah, I changed my mind once I got out."

"That's good," Calandra said. "At least that part is done."

Keisha and Fay went back downstairs. Fay still looked like she had just woke up. Calandra pulled her hair up in a bun to the side of her head while Keisha went back upstairs to find a better shoe.

"Here, try this one," Keisha said handing Fay a wedge sandal so she would be fly *and* comfortable at the club.

Keisha and Calandra stood back and looked at Fay.

"One last thing," Keisha said digging in her crocodile Prada bag and pulling out a tube of 'Oh Baby' and dabbing some on Fay's heart-shaped lips.

"Let's go," Calandra huffed.

The parking lot was packed when they pulled up. They spent 20 minutes looking for somewhere to park. The line snaked around the corner as the ladies approached the club.

"My feet already hurting," Calandra complained.

"I didn't realize people still be checking for the Go-Go like this," Keisha said.

"I hadn't been to a Go-Go in years," Fay said.

The three of them finally made it to the front of the club where they went through a metal detector, had their bags checked, and got patted down.

"Damn, is a bitch going to the club or to jail?" Calandra said snidely. "With all that and watch a muthafucker still get cut up in here."

"You complain too damn much," Keisha said. "Shut the fuck up!"

"I'm just saying . . ." Calandra reasoned.

The Go-Go was jam-packed with youngsters grinding and gyrating to Backyard Band. The dance floor was packed to capacity.

"I need a drink," Calandra said walking toward the bar.

"Come on girl, let me buy you a drink," Keisha said to Fay.

"They got wine coolers?"

"I doubt it. You stopped drinking or something?"

"I'm trying to," Fay said.

Calandra motioned for them to come to the bar.

"I just made some nigga buy us drinks," Calandra said. "What ya'll want?"

"I got a taste for something with Parrot Bay rum," Keisha said. "Fay said she stopped drinking."

"Bitch, what you want?" Calandra asked Fay ignoring Keisha.

Fay stood there trying to decide.

"She'll have a Fuzzy Navel," Calandra said to the bartender ordering for Fay.

The women stood at the bar drinking when a cutie walked up and ordered a few drinks for his crew.

"Wassup Mike?" Calandra purred.

"What's up with you, ma?"

"That depends on you."

"Is that right?"

"You already knowing."

He picked up his drinks and winked his eye at Calandra.

"Let me get these to my boys but make sure you get at me before you leave," he said.

"Who was that?" Fay asked?

"Girl, I know you know fine ass Mike Thompson of Lissen Band. Bitch, I thought you liked Go-Go?" Calandra said. "He's the lead vocalist and trumpet player of the group."

Fay and Keisha looked at each other and hunched their shoulders.

"Ain't that ole girl?" Calandra asked.

"Who you talking about now?" Keisha asked.

"The bitch Rell supposed to be fucking."

"Girl, we didn't come here for that," Keisha said.

Fay saw somebody she knew and walked off. Calandra kept eyeing in the direction of the girl who was supposed to be fucking her man. The heat in the club was becoming almost unbearable. Rare Essence segued into Chuck Brown. And the night was still young. Keisha turned around to the bar to get a bottle of water. The lights in the club came on. People started rushing toward the door.

"Oh shit!" Keisha said turning around and not seeing Calandra.

She could faintly hear her voice in the distance. It was moving further from her. When she finally made it outside the club, Calandra was fighting the chick she believed was fucking Rell. The girl pulled out a razor and cut Calandra on the arm. Calandra charged the girl and grabbed her by her hair.

"Don't call my house again bitch," Calandra said.

The girl spit in her face. Calandra threw her to the ground and started kicking her in the side and face. Keisha finally got to Calandra and grabbed her before security or the police were able to get to them.

"Damn bitch, didn't we talk about this?" Keisha asked.

"I didn't say shit if I recall correctly. You was doing all the talking," Calandra said breathing heavily.

"I don't know what to say about you."

"Don't say shit."

"But I'm going to because you always fucking somebody night up with yo' temper about Rell no-good ass," Keisha said.

"Fuck you Keisha!" Calandra yelled.

"You just don't fuckin' get it," Keisha said, walking off. "I gotta find Fay."

Fay had walked to the truck and was leaning up against it when they got there.

"Damn girl, I was looking for you," Keisha said. "How long you been out here?

"Since they cut the lights on in the club. What happened?" she asked looking at Calandra.

Keisha unlocked the doors. All three got in the truck.

"Here," Keisha said handing Calandra the container of Wet Wipes Antonio kept under the seat. "Don't drip no blood in this nigga truck because I'm not tryna hear his damn mouth."

Keisha dropped Fay off first.

"I know the night kinda got out of hand," Keisha said. "But we'll do something. I'll make it up to you."

"Girl, it's cool. I just needed to get out the house. Calandra, you may need to get that cut looked at," Fay said getting out the truck.

"I'm good," Calandra said.

"She was just being nice to you," Keisha said.

"Fuck her. I didn't want to go to no damn Go-Go in the first place."

"So now it's her fault that you got in a fight?" Keisha asked.

Calandra got quiet.

"You know what," she finally said. "You can let me out here. I'll walk."

Keisha brought the truck to a stop and unlocked the doors. Calandra got out. Keisha sped off.

17

You Don't Know My Name

"WHY YOU STILL being so secretive nigga?" Corey asked. "It's been weeks since we kicked it at the park and at my spot and I still don't know your name."

"So you gotta have my name to bust a nut with me?" the voice said over the phone.

"Obviously not but it would be nice to know who I'm fuckin around with."

"You don't need my name nigga. All you need is this dick," the masculine voice said.

"Oh word?"

"No doubt."

"So when can I get that?" Corey asked.

"When you want it?"

"Come through later tonight," Corey advised.

"Bet. I'll text you."

"Cool," Corey said hanging up the phone.

Rell and Antonio were already on the block when Corey got there.

"Wassup?" Corey said.

"Sup folk?" Antonio said eating a bag of Utz potato chips.

"Sup dawg," Rell said. "Where you been yo? We *been* out here."

"I was at the house helping Fay with some shit."

"How she doing?" Rell asked.

"She better, still a little depressed though."

"She get them flowers me and Keisha sent down there?" Antonio asked.

"Yeah, she love Cala Lilly's."

"What kind of lilies," Antonio asked.

"Calla Lilly's nigga."

"Only yo ass would know that," Rell joked.

"Oh son, I almost forgot. Keisha said bring her fuckin' Jennifer Hudson CD back up to the apartment," Antonio said.

"Shit, I ain't even dubbed it yet."

"Sounds personal slim. Get that chick her damn CD back though because I'm tired of hearing her fuckin' mouth."

"Alright, I'll run it up there later," Corey said. "The block seem madd dead yo."

"Pretty much," Rell said.

"Toot came by looking for you though," Antonio joked.

"Yeah right nigga."

"You do fuck around with just about anything," Rell said.

"Yo, don't start that gay shit today. I can't deal with it," Antonio said. "I'm about to break anyway. Ain't shit going on out here."

"Me too," Rell said.

Corey was walking back to the house when he received a text message – 'Have that ass ready nigga . . . Marcus.'

18

Put That Woman First

"**B**ABY, I FORGOT to tell you – your mother called yesterday while you were gone."

"Why the fuck you just telling me today then?" Antonio asked.

"I know you heard me say that I forgot. It was the *third* word in the sentence if you need to go back and review."

"Don't be cute Keisha. Did she say what she wanted?"

"Nope. She said to ask you to call home."

Antonio went back to watching *Jeopardy!*.

"Oh baby, another thing."

"What the fuck is it this time?" he looked up from the TV at her.

"Calandra going down to North Carolina to spend the 4th with Lil' Tony and thought it would be cool if everybody went down and hung out."

"What the fuck is in North Carolina?"

"That's where Calandra from."

"I know that much but what the fuck we gon' do down there on a holiday weekend? And who is everybody?"

"Me, you, Rell, Fay, Corey, and Calandra."

"Seems like drama and disaster to me," Antonio said.

"It'll be fun."

"What part of North Carolina?"

"Charlotte, Raleigh . . . fuck if I know," Keisha stammered. "It's all the same."

"*Jeopardy!* back on."

"What the fuck does that mean?"

"It was the *first* word of the sentence if you need to go back and review. So basically, shut the fuck up and we'll talk about that bullshit later."

"I don't know why you talk to me like that," Keisha said smacking her lips.

"Keisha, get yo ass out of here. Don't you and Baby Jane got somewhere ya'll need to be?"

"You ain't funny nigga," she said walking out the room. "And call yo' damn mama."

"Keisha," Antonio called her back.

"Oh so now you wanna talk?"

"Nah, but bring me a box of them Lorna Doone's out the cabinet when you come back."

Antonio finished watching *Jeopardy!* and grabbed his keys.

"You call yo mama?" Keisha asked handing Antonio a box of the shortbread cookies.

"Took you long enough."

"You could have gotten yo' lazy ass up and got them yourself."

Antonio picked up the cordless phone and dialed his mother's number. There was no answer.

"If my mama call back, tell her to hit me on my cell," Antonio said.

"Where you going?" Keisha asked.

"I'm a grown ass man. As you can see – my mama can't even keep up with me."

"The jury still out on that grown ass man part," Keisha retorted.

Antonio walked out of the apartment and noticed a silver Range Rover parked across the street. It stood out because he drove the flyest whips in his hood. He unlocked the doors of the Lexus and got in. He drove up Wisconsin Avenue to Chevy Chase and parked the car. He walked into Tiffany's.

"May we help you sir?" an older white man asked.

"Just looking right now."

"Very well. Let us know if we can assist you today."

Antonio walked around the store looking for nothing in particular. Smiling salespeople showed him watches from the Atlas collection and bangles designed by Elsa Peretti along with earrings and other trinkets.

"I'll take that," he said settling on a Paloma Picasso 100 carat pendant of smoky quartz in 18k gold.

The salesclerk wrapped the gift and handed Antonio the bag.

"Ain't this some shit," Antonio said looking at the ticket on his car. "If it ain't one thing."

Keisha was taking a nap when Antonio got back to the apartment. He sat the turquoise bag on the nightstand knowing that Keisha loved blue boxes – regardless of what was inside them. The mini collection of the boxes that she had amassed over the years and decorated the dresser with served as proof.

Keisha grew up in Anacostia which was not far from where she lived now. A daddy's girl so she was always in search of a man like her father. Her mother died of ovarian cancer when Keisha was in her pubescent years. The loss came right at the time when she needed a woman to tell her about training bras, feminine hygiene, how to be a lady, and how to treat her body.

Her father did the best he could. Taking her to Frederick Douglass House Museum often, which was in their neighborhood. They frequented the monuments and museums that littered D.C., they drove to Baltimore to the harbor on occasion, as well as frequent visits to local staples like Ben's Chili Bowl and the National Zoo.

Keisha's father wanted to make sure that she and her younger brother didn't miss out on anything because they had already missed knowing more about their mom. They were of modest means. Her father worked for the government as most people in the area did. Keisha kept a picture of her, her dad, and little brother in front of the White House on her nightstand.

Her father would also buy her nice things and show her that she deserved the best. She carried that into adulthood. She expected the best and Antonio more than provided her with that. He wasn't her father but he was her man.

Antonio's cell phone rang as he walked out the bedroom. "Heartless" by Kanye was the ring tone so he knew it was Rell. The similarities between the two was definitely not lost on Antonio. They were both metrosexual-*ish* and thought they rhymed better than they actually did.

"What the fuck you want nigga?"

"Yo you coming through on the block?"

"Damn son, when did I start answering to you?" Antonio asked.

"I'm just saying son. There has been a silver Range Rover rolling through a few times that nobody is familiar with. Shit seems suspect."

"Yo, I peeped that same truck earlier before I went out Maryland."

"What you go out there for?"

"Damn yo, get out my muthafuckin' business," Antonio said. "I'm on my way down there."

19

What About Us

"GIRL, YOU GON have to turn this Mary Mary or whoever this is off and put in some Mary J. Blige."

"Calandra, you in my truck. When we get you to the dealership to get yo' car, you can play whatever gon' get you through which is why I'm playing gospel."

"Well . . ."

"Exactly," Fay said turning up "The God in Me" so that it boomed in the truck.

"Did Keisha tell you about the plans to go to Charlotte for the 4th?"

"She mentioned it but she didn't go into any detail. Wassup?"

"I'm going down there to spend the holiday with my family and shit so I thought it would be cool if all of us went down there."

"Who is all of us?"

"Me, you, Rell, Keisha, Antonio, and Corey."

"How all of us getting down there? Where we staying? And what is there to do down there?" Fay asked all at once.

"Antonio's big ass Expedition. Either at my folk's house or get some rooms. And plenty," Calandra answered.

"I'll talk to Corey about it and see what he thinks," Fay said. "Isn't that the south? I've never been beyond Virginia going that way."

"First time for everything. It'll be cool."

"We're here so now you can get into your lil car and play Mary J., Diddy, or whoever you like."

"You damn straight," Calandra said slamming the door.

"You an ungrateful bitch," Fay said rolling down the window. "Don't ask me to do shit else for you."

"And you might as well be playing R. Kelly in that truck if you gon talk like that," Calandra said walking off. "Don't forget North Carolina for the 4th."

Calandra picked up her car and stopped by Keisha's on the way home.

"What you doing sleep at this time of day," Calandra asked.

"I was tired bitch," Keisha answered groggily and wiping sleep out of her eyes. "I guess yo' car fixed?"

"Yeah, Fay fat ass just took me to get it."

"What did I tell you about saying that shit. Stop that!"

"That bitch came for me today. I'm not thinking about her big-boned ass. Is that better?"

"You know you wrong. She didn't have to go out of her way to take you anywhere."

"Whatever. I told her about North Carolina for the 4th."

"What did she say?"

"I guess she gon' think about it. She said she was gon' talk it over with Corey. They can keep they asses here for all I care."

"You still need to tell me what we gon' do once we get there."

"We'll talk about that later but right now let's talk about what you done bought at Tiffany's," Calandra said spotting the bag.

"I ain't bought shit from Tiffany's lately."

"Well, where that bag come from?" Calandra asked pointing to it.

Keisha walked over to the nightstand and looked in the bag.

"Antonio must have bought this."

"Well, open it shit!" Calandra said.

"I don't know if its mine."

Once you open it and put whatever it is on – it's yours."

"Let me call him first," Keisha reasoned, picking up her phone.

"I'll call. You start opening the box," Calandra said snatching the phone.

"Wassup baby?" You get yo gift?" Antonio's voice oozed through the phone.

"It's yours!" Calandra said hanging up on Antonio. "What is it?"

Keisha slowly unwrapped the white bow tied around the blue box.

"Bitch, you taking too long," Calandra said.

"You act like it's yours," Keisha said.

"Just hurry up."

Keisha pulled the pendant from the box smiling.

"That's hot girl," Calandra said. "What you do to deserve that?"

"Put up with that nigga."

"I know that's right," Calandra said. "Hold up, let me look at that closer. Hand it here."

Keisha's phone started ringing.

"Why you hang up baby?"

"That was Calandra simple ass. She was calling for me to see if the Tiffany's bag was for me."

"You like it?"

"Hell yeah. Thank you."

"That's wassup. I just wanted you to know that a nigga appreciate you."

"Thank you baby."

"Your welcome," Antonio said. "Tell Calandra monkey ass that I'm gon' fuck her up for hanging up on me."

"Where you at anyway?"

"On the block. I'll be home later."

"If it's not too late, I may have a lil thank you gift," Keisha said, flirting on the phone while Calandra put the necklace around her neck.

"That's wassup," Antonio said ending the call.

"Bitch, I don't know what you done or what you plan to do but Antonio dropped about 6 G's for this!" Calandra shouted.

"How you know," Keisha asked.

"I was on the Tiffany site and priced the amethyst one," she answered. "Let me find out you giving it to 'Tonio like *that!*"

"Bitch, get out my house!" Keisha laughed, toying with her new something special as it dangled from her neck.

"Well girl, I'm about to go on to the house. Did Antonio say whether or not Rell was with him?" Calandra asked.

"Nah, he didn't say"

"I'll call you later."

"Aiiight."

Calandra rolled through the spot where Antonio and the crew hung out and saw Rell standing out there.

"Rell!" she hollered, slowing the car down to a crawl. "Come here."

"Gon' over there and see what that bitch want?" Corey said.

"Watch yo' mouth," Rell said.

"Sup baby?" Rell said once he got to the car.

"Nothing. What gay ass Corey say when you was walking over here?"

"He ain't say shit."

"I know he said something but I'll catch up with his ass in a minute."

"Calandra, cut that shit out. Why you beefin with that nigga?"

"'Cause he want what I got."

"If you got it, why you worried? Stop feeding into them bullshit rumors," Rell said. "You know how the fuck I get down."

"When you coming home so we can get down then?"

"You headed there now?"

"Yeah."

"I can roll now then. Aint shit going on out here."

"Well tell yo lil playmates bye and lets go."

"I see you got jokes," Rell said walking back over to his boys.

"You out son?" Antonio asked.

"Cruella De Vil making him come home," Corey said laughing.

"Don't get fucked up Corey," Rell said.

"Nigga, go on home with that trick," Corey said.

"Make that yo last negative comment nigga," Rell said walking back to Calandra's car.

"So what ya'll been doing all day?" Calandra asked once they got in the house.

"Shit. You know that street hustle. A whole bunch of down time. Out there smoking, drinking, joking, and shit."

"So why you be out there?"

"Ain't shit else to do."

"When you gon' do something with yourself?"

"Shit, when you do I guess," Rell said laughing.

"I do something nigga. So me doing braids ain't doing nothing?"

"I mean it's cool but you only do that shit when you feel like it here at the apartment. It ain't like it's a real job."

"It's real enough nigga. Like I said, what you gon' do?"

"Rap."

"What?"

"You heard me. I'm gon' be a rapper."

"I see," Calandra said folding clothes. "Every nigga in the hood wanna rap or play basketball. What the fuck make you special? Do you know how many dudes out here tryna do that shit?"

"Every nigga don't spit like me though . . .

Flyest dude on the planet/ my girl sexier than Janet
But yo dude ain't JD/ that honor goes to me
Just tryna hold you down/ maximize this chemistry we found
Hot like the heat this season/ if you feel it – let that be the reason
I thought we came home to fuck/ but it looks like you stuck

"Baby, I'm not saying yo shit not hot or that I won't support you. I'm just saying be realistic."

"Now you starting to piss me off."

"For having your best interest in mind?"

"For shitting on a nigga's dreams. It's hard enough out here in the streets without a nigga having someone who got his back," Rell said.

"Rell, you blowing this all out of proportion."

"Am I?"

"Yes, you are."

Thought a bitch was on my team/ but she into killing dreams
No different from the haters in the street/ So, with that – you can beat yo feet
Fucked up how you dogging a nigga/ just open yo mouth when I pull the trigger
You overpriced like Abercrombie & Fitch/ as a matter-of-fact, you just a bitch

Rell walked toward the door.

"Where the fuck you going Rell? I know yo little rhyme wasn't directed at me," Calandra said.

Rell walked out the apartment on his way back up the block.

"Don't bother coming back tonight," she yelled after him. "Find somewhere else to sleep."

20

As We Lay

RELL WOKE UP laying beside Corey.
"What time is it yo?" Rell asked.

"Too muthafuckin' early to be talking and asking questions," Corey said.

"What the fuck happened last night?"

"Didn't shit happen nigga except you coming back up on the block with yo' face long talking about how Calandra fake ass was shitting on yo dreams."

"How the fuck I end up over here?"

"We was out there blazing and shit and you said ole girl told you not to come home so I told you to crash over here. We got in this morning, drank a Heineken or two, blazed one last blunt, and went to sleep nigga."

"Damn, how I forget all that?"

"Nigga, I don't know but I'm too fuckin sleepy to care."

"Corey," Fay knocked on the door.

"Yo, hold up."

"What you doing?" she asked. "You dressed?"

"Nah, I'm not. What you need?"

"Calandra just called asking if Rell was up here."

"Why the fuck would Rell be over here?"

"Hell, if I know."

"I'm about to go run some errands. I'll see you when I get back," Fay said.

"Aiiight."

"Good looking out," Rell said.

"Nigga, take yo ass home," Corey said.

Corey's cell phone started ringing.

"Who calling you this early?" Rell asked reaching for the phone.

"Yo girl at home nigga. You don't run shit here."

"You don't think?" Rell said snatching Corey's phone from his hand.

Corey tried to get the phone back before Rell could answer it.

"Hello," Rell said.

"You up?" the voice asked.

"I am now," Rell answered in Corey's phone.

"You sound different."

"I'm just waking up," Rell said holding Corey at bay.

"We should get up today if you not busy."

"I ain't got shit planned."

"Once you get yourself together, holla at me so we can see wassup."

"Aiiight bet," Rell said hanging up the phone.

"Why the fuck you do that?" Corey asked finally getting the phone back.

"I guess you got a date today," Rell said. "Who the fuck was that anyway?"

"How am I supposed to know? You talked to them."

"You should know who calling you. How many niggas you got calling you?"

"Not enough," Corey shoot back.

"That's the shit I'm talking about. You know that's foul."

"Rell, you not my nigga."

"Yo, I just hope you not still fucking around with dude I caught you with 'cause Antonio said he seen dude somewhere and he didn't have a good feeling about him."

"It ain't for Antonio to feel," Corey said laughing.

"Just watch yo muthafuckin' back," Rell said putting his shorts and shirt on with his drop socks and black Nike boots. The nigga was so D.C. he didn't even realize no one was really checkin for Alldâz anymore.

"Tell Calandra I said wassup," Corey said rolling back over in the bed.

21

Ridin'

COREY GRABBED THE bath towel as he stepped out the shower. He stood in the mirror and brushed his teeth with the oversized white towel wrapped around his waist. He heard his phone beeping which meant he had a text message.

'Wassup wit you?' the message read.

'Just getting out the shower,' Corey texted back.

Corey dried off and looked in his closet for something to wear. His phone beeped.

'I should be there licking you dry.'

'Damn straight,' Corey texted.

He grabbed a red Ron Herman t-shirt, a pair of khaki gap cargo shorts, and some Creative Recreations out the box.

'I'm outside yo' spot,' the message read.

Corey looked out the window and saw a silver Range Rover.

'Give me two minutes,' he texted.

"This muthafucker is fly," Corey said getting in the expensive utility vehicle.

"Glad you like it."

"So Marcus . . ." Corey paused for effect after saying the name.

"Sup slim?"

"Why was I always seeing you on the train if you got this to roll in?" Marcus laughed.

"Gas ain't no joke. Filling this bitch up is a problem."

"I feel you," Corey said. "What's the game plan? Where we headed?"

"I figure we ride a minute. Maybe blow some smoke."

"Cool."

"So what you be up to besides freaking in the park?

"That was one time," Corey said defensively.

"I'm just fucking with you."

"I guess a nigga just be on some hood shit for real. You know how it is out here. Niggas just hustlin' they lives away on the corner and shit."

"True."

"But a nigga like me got some other shit planned. I'm tryna get back in school up at Howard next Spring and shit. Or possibly UDC if my money ain't right but I gotta get in somewhere."

"That's a good look."

Marcus' Range Rover crossed over the Maryland line when he pulled a half an ounce from a small, concealed compartment in the truck.

"Roll this up," he said. "It should be some Chocolate-flavored Philly's in the console.

Corey rolled two blunts and sat one in the drink tray. He pushed in the truck's cigarette lighter. It popped out. Corey lit the blunt and tilted his head back, inhaling the smoke.

"Pretty good shit you got here yo."

"I thought you might like it," Marcus said.

Corey took another deep inhale and passed the blunt to Marcus.

"Yo, pull over at this WaWa," Corey said.

"What the fuck is WaWa?"

"It's like 7 Eleven on steroids yo. I haven't been to one in a minute but it's a beast. You want something out of here?"

"Just grab me a bag of chips, a Mr. Goodbar, and a Lipton Iced Tea," Marcus said handing Corey a $50 bill.

"Bet."

Corey got back in the truck with two bags full of shit.

"Damn yo, you bought groceries didn't you?"

"Don't know when I'll get back to a WaWa yo," Corey said laughing.

The ride back to D.C. was mostly quiet as both men were feeling the high.

"You wanna smoke another one?" Marcus asked.

"Nah, I'm good."

"The 4th coming up and shit. What you got planned?"

"I think my crew rolling down to North Carolina or somewhere down south and shit."

"How long ya'll gone be down there?"

"Couple days."

"That's wassup."

"What you doing?"

"Haven't decided yet. I'm sure something will come up."

"No doubt."

Marcus' truck pulled up in front of Corey's.

"Holla at me before you bounce down south."

"I got you," Corey said.

Corey opened the door, grabbed the WaWa bags, and walked in the house. Marcus pulled out his Blackberry and texted 'Them niggas rolling down south for the 4th. I think I'm gonna set Phase I in motion while they're gone.'

Marcus pulled off. The response message on his phone read: 'MAKE IT HAPPEN' in all caps.

22

I Should Have Cheated

"SOMEBODY CALL RELL and Calandra and tell them to come on," Antonio said loading up the Escalade Hybrid he had just purchased or rather traded the Expedition for. It was a beautiful truck – Infrared with peanut butter-colored, leather seats. Three TV's, voice navigation, refrigeration, monogrammed headrests, and other details 'Tonio had customized filled his new toy. He was more than ready to put it on the road and put a few miles on it.

Keisha grabbed her yellow Fendi bag from the front seat and pulled her cell phone out of it. She had nicknamed the bag Tweety.

"Where the fuck are you?

"Bitch, I'm pulling up now," Calandra said.

Rell got out and started getting luggage out of the trunk.

"Where the fuck ya'll think we going? Europe?" Antonio asked. "Calandra, we're going to fuckin' North Carolina for less than a week and you packed like you gon' be gone for a month or better."

"I gotta have options," she said handing Antonio the last of her Diane Von Furstenberg luggage.

Antonio shook his head. "Let's go," he yelled.

Corey, Fay, Rell, Calandra, Keisha, and Antonio all jumped in the truck for the six hour road trip.

"You get the cooler?" Keisha asked.

"Yeah," Antonio answered.

"You got a radar detector?" Rell asked.

"Yeah," Antonio answered.

"You know where you going?" Calandra asked.

"Yeah," Antonio answered agitated.

"You ain't gotta yell nigga," Calandra said. "Here, put this in."

"What's on this?" Antonio asked taking the unmarked CD.

"It's a mix CD."

"Who on it?"

"Some of everybody. Just put it in."

"Oh, I got yo Jennifer Hudson CD too Keisha," Corey said.

"It's about time nigga. You had it long enough."

"I got some gospel," Fay said.

"Okay," Antonio said disinterested.

Three mix CD's later, they pulled over in Clarksville, VA for gas. Everybody got out but Keisha who was sleeping. Antonio pumped the gas. Fay went to get snacks. Calandra was on the side of the truck talking to her mother on the phone. Rell and Corey went to the restroom.

"You bring some green?" Corey asked from the urinal beside Rell.

"Hell yeah nigga. I'm gon need it dealing with all ya'll asses all weekend. I should grab some Dutches though."

"Where the fuck we staying anyway?"

"Calandra said she was gon ask her people if everybody could crash at they house," Rell said.

"I doubt that shit work."

"Me too," Rell laughed. "You let yo' boyfriend know you was going out of town?"

"I don't have a muthafuckin' boyfriend."

"Yeah, I hear you."

Corey walked back to the truck while Rell bought blunts. Calandra and Fay were already in the truck.

"You a slow assed nigga," Antonio said to Rell when he re-joined the group.

"You tryna smoke, right?"

"Hell yeah!"

"Well, shut the fuck up then," Rell said. "I had to buy some more blunts."

"I hope ya'll not gon' be smoking that shit in this truck," Fay said.

"Pass it to me once ya'll light it up," Calandra said talking over Fay.

"I'll put one of your gospel CD's in if you cool with us smoking a blunt or two," Antonio bartered with Fay.

"What kind of trade-off is that," she asked.

"Just hand me a CD."

Fay handed him KeKe Sheard while Rell rolled three blunts. The truck filled with smoke quickly once Rell put the blunts in rotation.

"This some good shit," Corey said.

"It blow like some shit I had earlier in the week. Where you get this?"

"Jermaine. I'm telling you that nigga have the best shit," Rell said.

"And I'm telling you to stop fucking wit that nigga," Antonio said pulling on one of the blunts. "But it is good shit."

"Keisha ass been knocked out almost since we got in the fuckin truck," Calandra said over KeKe's voice. "Pass the damn blunt Antonio."

"I know. She been sleeping a lot lately," Antonio said. "Fay, this CD ain't half bad Ma."

Once they got to North Carolina, Calandra helped Antonio get to her parents house.

"Ya'll got a lil farm and everything," Corey said looking at the horses and cows on the land.

"This some country shit," Antonio said.

"Shut up nigga and put that blunt out," Calandra said.

"It ain't like they ain't gon' smell it in our clothes," Rell said.

"Ain't nobody said shit to you," she responded.

"Baby get up," Antonio said shaking Keisha. "We here."

Lil' Tony ran out the house and jumped in Calandra's arms. Her mother and father followed shortly behind him.

"Wassup Tony?" Calandra asked the young boy. "You missed mommy?'

"Did you come to get me?" he asked.

"Not yet but I am gon' be here for a few days."

"When am I going back home?"

"I'm coming back to get you right before school starts back so just a few more weeks," Calandra said.

"Ya'll come on in," Calandra's father said.

They all introduced themselves to Calandra's parents while her mother made them all glasses of iced tea.

"How long ya'll staying?" her father asked.

"Just the weekend sir," Corey said.

"Well make yourselves at home. Katharine will show you where you can sleep once you get settled in."

"Thank you," they all said.

"Where is Jeremy, Mama?" Calandra asked.

"Somewhere chasing a skirt," she said. "That's one mannish boy. If he ain't on the phone with some lil girl, he at her house, or they over here. He ain't sat still since he been down here."

"I bet," Calandra said. "I'll call his cell phone later."

"I'm about to go to the market. Ya'll need anything in particular?" Mrs. Katharine asked.

"No," they all said.

"That's no *ma'am*," she said grabbing her handbag and walking out the door.

Calandra showed everyone around her childhood home.

"This is nice," Fay said.

"Yo hood ass grew up here?" Antonio asked.

"Nigga, fuck you!" Calandra said.

"See, that's what I mean," Antonio laughed.

"Whatever," she said.

"What we doing tonight?" Keisha asked.

"Club Ice be jumping on Friday nights plus it's a holiday weekend so it should be extra crunk," Calandra said.

"What's the dress code?" Corey asked.

"You can wear jeans as long as you dress them up. No athletic gear or gym shoes," she said.

Calandra's father, Mr. Spencer, was milking a cow when Calandra took the group outside.

"That's some gangsta backwoods shit right there," Antonio said.

"You ain't lying," Rell said.

"You'll be pouring that over your cereal in the morning," Calandra said.

"I'll pass on that," Antonio said. "Rell, we might as well grab these bags while we out here."

Corey followed the women back into the house while Antonio and Rell walked to the truck.

"Yo dawg," Rell said. "Maybe we should only stay the night here and get rooms tomorrow."

"Why you say that? This yo' girl spot. Yo future in-laws," Antonio said.

"I'm just sayin, niggas gon' be tryna fuck and smoke and shit. I figure it better if we don't do that here."

"I feel you but are you helping to pay for the room's nigga?"

"I mean, I can," Rell said.

"You *can* and you *will*. Go tell them to come get what they need for tonight so I don't have to tote all this shit in there."

All of the guys had taken showers and were dressed. Keisha and Calandra showered together to save time and Fay was downstairs talking to Mrs. Katharine.

"Yo, Keisha 'nem done. Go tell Fay to come on and jump in the shower," Antonio said.

"She not going," Corey said.

"Why not?" Rell asked.

"She said she didn't feel like it," Corey said.

Calandra and Keisha took what seemed like an eternity deciding what to wear to the club. When the last spray of Sarah Jessica Parker's *Lovely* met Keisha's neck and Calanda had rubbed Kiehl's Crème De Corps body lotion into her elbows and arms, the clique jumped in the truck. Antonio ejected Fay's gospel CD. Rell immediately started rolling a blunt and Corey checked messages on his phone.

"What's the radio station out here?" Antonio asked.

"Power 98," Calandra said.

Mr. Incognito was broadcasting live from the club they were headed to.

"I bet these hoes country as shit down here," Antonio said.

"That shouldn't matter to you," Keisha said punching him in his arm.

"That just mean they thick as shit," Rell said.

"Don't get fucked up Rell," Calandra snapped.

"Please don't get her started," everyone said.

"Ya'll ain't cute," Calandra said.

Antonio pulled up to the front of the club and valeted. They all jumped out and got in line.

"This might be alright," Corey said.

"It's some potential," Antonio echoed.

Two obviously gay dudes walked by.

"Looks like they even got a little something for you too Corey," Rell joked.

"Whatever son!" Corey said.

"Play nice boys," Keisha interjected.

They got inside the club and Antonio started a tab for the group. Everybody ordered their favorite drinks. One R&B song lent itself to another with Hip Hop and Reggae mixed in. Corey was in a corner in some chick's face. Rell and Antonio held the bar up. Keisha and Calandra danced with each other on the dance floor.

"This ain't bad girl," Keisha said.

"I told you it was gon be cool," Calandra said.

"It's some fine muthafuckers in here too," Keisha said.

"Don't forget the ballers," Calandra added.

"I gotta go to the restroom. Come on," Keisha said.

"Rell said we was getting rooms in the morning," Calandra said re-applying her make-up in the mirror.

"Yeah, Antonio mentioned that," Keisha said coming out of the stall.

"Get that piece of tissue from under your shoe before we leave this bathroom," Calandra laughed.

"*Restrooms* are public facilities," Keisha said removing the tissue from her heel and washing her hands. "A *bathroom* is at your house."

"Yeah, yeah whatever!"

They walked out of the restroom, heading back to the dance floor.

"That's my shit," Keisha said as Incognito spun "Want it, Need it" by Plies and Ashanti.

"I know the fuck he ain't," Calandra said.

"What's wrong?" Keisha asked bopping her head.

"Look over by the bar," Calandra said already walking in that direction.

"Fuck!" Keisha said.

Before she could catch up to Calandra, her friend had some girl's neck in her hands.

"What the fuck you think I'm doing?" Calandra asked.

"Let me go," the girl pleaded.

"Calandra, fall back," Rell said grabbing her.

"Get yo' muthafuckin' hands off me," she said.

It took Antonio, Rell, and Keisha to get Calandra to release the girl and calm down.

"Find Corey so we can go," Antonio said.

"Fuck that! I'm tryna have fun. Calandra not fucking my night up," Keisha said. "Bitch done that twice in the last month."

Keisha and Antonio walked out on the dance floor. Calandra and Rell walked outside.

"If you wasn't tryna holla, then why the fuck was you all in her face?" Calandra asked.

"She thought she knew me," he said. "She thought I was some nigga she had fucked around with."

"You gotta come better than that."

"If I come any other way, I'll be lying."

"You lying now."

"There you go. Come on baby. You think I'm crazy enough to be hollering at some chick with yo volatile ass up in the same place?"

"I would think you got better sense."

"Give me a kiss," Rell said leaning in toward her.

Calandra turned away from him.

"We not straight nigga," she said sulking.

"Awww Boo Boo, come here."

They went back in the club and joined Keisha and Antonio on the dance floor.

"You two good?" Keisha asked Calandra.

"We cool," she answered.

"You straight?" Antonio asked Rell.

He nodded his head yeah. Corey walked up to Antonio and said that he was leaving with the chick he had been talking to all night.

"Oh word?" Antonio asked with both surprise in his eyes and his voice.

"Yeah nigga," Corey said.

"Do you homeboy," Antonio said.

"Always," Corey said walking off.

The rest of the crew all went to Waffle House before arriving at Calandra's parent's house at 4 in the morning.

23

Southern Hospitality

COREY KNOCKED ON The Spencer's door around 9 a.m. the next morning.

"I guess you got lost?" Mrs. Katharine joked.

"Something like that," Corey said.

"Well go wake the others and tell them I got breakfast prepared down here.

"Cool."

"That would be 'yes ma'am,'" she said.

Everyone came downstairs to a breakfast of various cereal, sausage links and patties, cheese eggs, grits, ham, bacon, toast, biscuits, strawberry and peach preserves, milk, water, and orange juice.

"Happy 4th of July!" Mrs. Katharine said. "What ya'll got planned for the day?"

"I thought it would be good to take them to Carowinds," Calandra answered.

"That sounds like a good idea," Mrs. Katharine said.

"Damn, I'm full," Corey said dropping his fork on his plate.

"Corey!" Calandra exclaimed. "Watch yo' mouth!"

"Oh, my bad Mr. and Mrs. Spencer. Breakfast was delicious though."

"I'm glad you enjoyed it young man," Mrs. Katharine said. "Let's go Henry and leave these youngsters be."

"I know that's not the milk from yesterday in that pitcher," Antonio said.

"Nah nigga. It's got to be pasteurized first. That's probably from last week," Calandra said laughing.

"I can't even front. It was good and cold," he said.

"Corey, what you end up getting into last night?" Keisha asked.

"A threesome."

Fay, Calandra, and Keisha stopped clearing the dishes. Rell almost choked.

"With the girl you left with and who?" Calandra asked.

"Her boyfriend," Corey said handing his plate to Fay to put in the sink.

"Yo, that's too much," Antonio said leaving the room.

"I know her *and* her boyfriend from high school," Calandra said. "He ain't gay."

"He was last night."

"Who knew?" Calandra stated. "That nigga was fine as hell in school."

"Still is," Corey said pulling out his camera phone to show her a picture.

"Damn! Keisha, come look at this shit," Calandra said.

"What are you all doing in this picture right here?" Keisha asked.

"I'm licking her pussy while he fucks me," Corey said taking the phone to see which picture she was referring to.

"Some hoes will do *anything* to keep a nigga," Calandra said wiping off the table.

"But most hoes do what they were *already* going to do anyway," Corey said.

Fay left out the room. Rell looked Corey dead in his face.

"Come here Rell," Calandra said.

"I ain't looking at that bullshit," he said. "Ya'll need to hurry up so we can get checked into this hotel."

Almost every hotel in the city was booked for the weekend. They were finally able to get three rooms at the Hampton Inn. Corey and Rell got the bags out the truck. Antonio paid for the rooms while the girls looked around the lobby.

"What's wrong with you?" Corey asked.

Rell was quiet. He sat the bags down and stared Corey in his face again, looking for something he wasn't owed and wasn't going to get – remorse.

"I'm through fucking with you. I see you on anything moving," Rell finally said.

"I guess that's why you and Calandra got into it last night – cause you not? Nigga, you do the same shit," Corey countered.

Rell picked up the bags and walked into the hotel lobby.

"That's what I thought," Corey said to himself.

Antonio gave Fay a room key for her and Corey. He handed Rell a keycard for him and Calandra.

"All the rooms are on the third floor," he said.

Everybody jumped on the elevator. Calandra's phone rang.

"Hello," she said. "Let me call you back Mama. I'm in the elevator."

"What did your mother say about us leaving?" Keisha asked.

"She was a little disappointed. She likes doing for people but she'll get over it."

"Your mother is real nice Calandra," Fay said. "We talked for a long time last night."

"She told me," Calandra said as the elevator door opened. "Don't forget that we going to Carowinds so don't take all day."

Within the hour, they were on I-77 headed to the water park.

"Did you check to see if Jeremy and Lil' Tony wanted to come?" Keisha asked lowering the music.

"Jeremy's mother is up here, too. They're all meeting us there," Calandra said.

"That's your first cousin?" Keisha asked.

"Nah, she my second and we not that cool but I fucks with Jeremy and he's like a big brother to Lil' Tony so I deal with her stupid ass. She just moved to DC 'cause I did."

"Ain't nobody in their right mind followed you nowhere," Antonio joked.

"I'm being serious," Calandra said. "You always on joke time."

Corey reached in the back and grabbed a bottled water out of the cooler. There was a ring. Everyone checked their phone. It was Corey's.

"What's good?" he answered.

"We made it down yesterday."

"Tomorrow."

"I'll text you when I get back."

Everyone in the truck was trying to decipher the one-sided conversation they had just heard as well as wondering who was on the other end.

"Who you telling yo' business to?" Rell asked.

"Not Rell," Corey said.

"Nigga, I'm just saying. Don't be putting all of our business out there," Rell said. "You getting real fuckin' sloppy with your new pieces."

"Pieces? Nigga, what the fuck you *think* you talking about?"

"All these fuck buddies you being so open with," Rell said.

The truck was silent. Everyone was waiting for someone to say something.

"Like I said, you *think* you know what you talking about."

"Would you two cut that bitch shit out," Antonio said.

Calandra was biting her tongue trying to keep from saying something. The amusement park was 10 minutes away. The group was getting antsy. Doors began opening on the truck before Antonio could even park.

"Damn, it's hot out here," Keisha said.

"Perfect weather for a water park," Calandra said.

Calandra and Keisha caught up with Lil' Tony and the rest of Calandra's family. Antonio, Corey, Rell, and Fay wanted to get on Drop Zone.

"Mama, can we go to the Scooby Doo Haunted Mansion?" Lil' Tony asked.

"We sure can. Let's go."

"Girl, I'm feeling light-headed," Keisha said. "I'm about to find somewhere to sit down."

"You alright?" Calandra asked.

"I'm fine. It's just the heat."

"Aiight, we'll be back in a few. I'm gonna take Lil' Tony to the Haunted Mansion and to Dodg'ems."

The group met back up and they all rode the Carolina Cyclone and Vortex with the exception of Keisha who waited with Lil' Tony and his young cousins at the exit points.

"You sure you okay baby?" Antonio asked.

"I'm alright," Keisha said.

"You don't look alright. I'm about to tell everyone that we about to go. It's getting late anyway."

They stopped at Olive Garden and ate before going back to the hotel. Everyone ended up in one room smoking, playing cards, and watching DVD's. Fay was in and out of the room because of the weed smoke. Calandra had gone back to her parent's house to spend time with her son.

"This wasn't a bad lil trip," Antonio said.

"I definitely have enjoyed myself," Corey said.

Everyone laughed.

"I bet you have nigga," Rell said.

"I think I ate too much," Keisha said lying across the bed. "Can you go get me something to settle my stomach baby?"

"Nah, I'll stay here with you but Rell and Corey can take the truck and go get something," Antonio said volunteering his boys.

"That's cool. We need some more blunts anyway," Rell said. "Where are the keys?"

"Look in my jeans lying on that chair by the window," Antonio said.

It was about 9:30 p.m. when Rell and Corey left the hotel. They found a gas station that had Pepto-Bismol as well as some Green Honey Dutch's.

"You haven't said much to a nigga this whole weekend outside of yo lil jokes," Corey said.

"Wasn't shit to say," Rell responded.

"I don't even understand you son."

"Ain't shit to understand."

They were on their way back to the hotel when Rell pulled off the main street and drove a mile or so down a dark country road.

"Where the fuck you going?" Corey asked.

"Nigga, sit back and let me drive."

Rell pulled over to the side of the narrow road and threw the truck in park, turning the lights out.

"Get out the fuckin truck!"

"For what nigga?" Corey asked. "I don't even know where the fuck we are."

"Just get the fuck out the truck."

They both got out and Rell walked around to the passenger side. He grabbed Corey by the throat and choked him. At the same time, putting his tongue in his mouth. Corey's whole body went limp. Rell unbuckled his belt and unzipped his jeans with his free hand. He allowed his jeans to fall to his ankles. Corey pulled down Rell's navy blue basketball shorts and his stripped boxer shorts. Rell's dick was brick. Corey lowered himself and found Rell's dick which he instantly swallowed.

Rell cocked his head to the side and closed his eyes. He heard his cell phone ringing by his ankles and felt the vibration. Corey inhaled Rell's entire shaft. He released it from his mouth and began licking under his balls. He took both in his mouth simultaneously. Rell's phone rang again. He bent to grab it and answered it.

"Where the fuck ya'll at?" Antonio demanded. "Get the fuck back here now," his voice boomed through the phone.

It was 10:15 p.m. when they walked back in the room everyone had been chilling in earlier. Bags were packed and unease had settled on faces.

"We gotta go back to D.C . . . . *now!*" Antonio said.

24

What Means The World To You

CALANDRA HUGGED HER parents and kissed Lil' Tony on the front porch.

"I'll see you in a few weeks, she said to the young boy with tears in his eyes. Be a big boy and wipe those tears."

"He'll be alright," Mr. Spencer said patting the boy on his back.

"I'll call ya'll when we make it back."

"Okay, be careful," Mrs. Katharine said.

There was an eerie stillness in the truck when Calandra got in.

"Why we leaving today? I thought we were staying until tomorrow night?"

No one said anything as Antonio backed out the drive.

"What's wrong with ya'll?" Calandra asked.

"Someone shot up Antonio's mother's house," Keisha finally offered.

"Damn! Is she okay?" Calandra asked.

"Fortunately, she wasn't there when it happened," Keisha said drinking the Pepto-Bismol from the bottle.

"Antonio, you know who did it?" Calandra asked.

"Nah, but I will when we get back," he said.

"Niggas getting bold out here."

"Niggas been bold," Antonio said. "They got the right nigga this time though."

Everyone had gone to sleep but Antonio and Fay. He looked in the rearview and saw her gazing out the window.

"You can get some rest Fay. I'm cool," Antonio said.

"I'm fine," she said. "I just got a lot on my mind. I'm not sleepy though."

"Do you have anymore of those gospel CD's with you?"

Fay handed him Smokie Norful. Antonio had repeated "I Need You Now" eight times by the time they crossed into the District of Columbia.

Antonio was his mother's baby boy. Her favorite, raised in a strict, Christian home; he rebelled early on. The lore of the streets rang louder in his ear than the organ pipes in the church where his mother was an usher and choir director and his father was a deacon.

Antonio was brewing with revenge. His relationship with his mother was beyond special. The fact that someone had threatened her life was unfathomable. Antonio was seeing red.

The sun was coming up and one by one, the group began waking up.

"Call me when you ready to make moves," Rell said grabbing all his and Calandra's bags.

"Will do," Antonio said.

"I'll be praying that no more violence comes out of this," Fay said to Antonio.

"You do that," he said. "Can I hold on to this CD?"

"Of course," she said.

"Ring the cell," Corey said.

"No doubt."

Antonio drove straight to his Aunt's house where his mother was staying. She was understandably upset.

"Have you seen the house," Antonio's mother asked.

"No, I came straight here. Did you contact the police?"

"Your aunt took care of all that. They came out and asked a lot of questions and said they would be looking into it, investigating and whatever."

Keisha stayed with Antonio's aunt and mother while he went to look at the house. Several windows were shot completely out in the front as well as holes in the door from the bullets. Antonio could tell that two kinds of guns were used – a Desert Eagle and a Glock.

"Call Corey and tell him to be on the block at our usual time," Antonio said to Rell.

"Yo, wassup?"

"Just do what the fuck I asked you," he said hanging up.

The cops later came by and questioned Antonio and Keisha at the apartment.

"They ain't gon do shit!" Antonio said as the officers left.

"They might," Keisha responded.

"This is DC. They don't give a fuck about a house being shot up in the hood."

Keisha cooked spaghetti while Antonio watched *Jeopardy!*. Day became night. Corey, Rell, and Antonio met up on the block.

"I need you two to be my eyes and ears on the street. See what the fuck is being said. Somebody knows who is responsible for my mom shit getting shot up," Antonio said.

"You know we got you," Rell said.

"Consider it done," Corey said.

"I can't even believe some nigga out here would have the false sense of security to even entertain what they did," Antonio said.

"Don't sweat it yo," Rell said.

"How the fuck the explosives go off at my mom crib on the 4th?" Antonio tried to reason. "How ironic is that?"

25

Friend of Mine

"WHAT THE LINES say bitch?" Calandra asked from the other side of the bathroom door.

Keisha walked out the bathroom.

"*Two* pink," she said.

"You pregnant bitch!" Calandra laughed.

"Girl, that ain't funny. I don't want no fuckin' kids right now."

"Looks like you don't have a choice."

"Oh, I have a choice."

"I know you ain't thinking about having an abortion," Calandra said.

Keisha just looked at her.

"Fuck that girl. That's not even an option."

"For who?"

"For you," Calandra said. "Don't do that shit plus you haven't even talked it over with Antonio."

"Who said I was going to?"

"Bitch, that's wrong," Calandra said.

"You better not say shit to anybody," Keisha said. "I gotta decide how I'm gonna handle this. The first being making an appointment with my doctor to be certain."

"True," Calandra agreed.

"That's why yo ass been sleeping so much and feeling light-headed."

"I guess so," Keisha said.

"Girl, we was doing a lot of smoking on that trip. I hope it didn't affect the baby."

"You and me both."

"Call me if you need anything. Oh, whatever happened with Antonio's mama's house?"

"The police are still investigating and you know Antonio and them doing their Sherlock Holmes in the street as well."

"Yeah, Rell has been consumed with finding out," Calandra said.

"That *is* Antonio's best friend. Antonio's mother is like his mother. You know how that is."

"You know I do. Rell, would rather be looking in Antonio's face than mine. So, you know I know."

"Girl, don't take it personal. You know how men are."

"I know. Look, call me," Calandra said leaving. "I got a baby shower to plan."

"Calandra, I told you not to say shit until I know for sure."

"I heard that part," Calandra said. "I also heard the part when you said that you had *two* pink lines."

"That test can have errors."

"The same errors as you sleeping all the time, being dizzy, and ordering crazy shit when we out eating?"

"All that can just be a stomach virus," Keisha said.

"Or a baby in the stomach," Calandra said closing the door in Keisha's face.

26

The Arms Of The One Who Loves You

KEISHA WAITED IN the small, sterile room for her results, secretly praying that the EPT she took at home was wrong.

"Congratulations, you're 7 weeks pregnant," her OB/GYN said walking into the room with the results on the clipboard.

They spent the next 30 minutes in consultation about how she needed to care for herself to ensure a healthy baby and scheduling follow-up visits.

"You don't seem all that happy Ms. Riley," her doctor noticed.

"Just a lot on my mind," she said solemnly.

"Well, you do know that your mood affects the baby so try to cheer up a bit."

She was in the bed when Antonio came home. He attempted to get in the bed without waking her.

"Baby, is that you?"

"Yeah, go back to sleep," Antonio said.

"We need to talk," Keisha said turning over and turning on the lamp.

"What's wrong?"

"I'm pregnant."

Antonio's eyes lit up as he grabbed Keisha and hugged her.

"Is it a boy?" he patted her stomach.

"I just found out today nigga," she laughed. "It's too soon to tell."

"Damn baby!"

"I didn't know you were going to be so excited."

"Why wouldn't I be?" he asked.

"Because we haven't discussed kids since I was 15."

"That was a long time ago baby. Things are different now."

"I just don't know if I can take losing another child."

"You can't think like that," Antonio said.

"And what if we do bring a child into this world? Then what?"

"Then we provide for him."

"*Him?*"

"Every nigga wants a son," Antonio said. "You gotta keep the bloodline going."

"Anyway, Calandra and I were talking awhile back and its hard raising kids today, *especially* boys."

"It may be hard but its not impossible."

"I don't know if I want to keep it," Keisha said softly.

"Keisha, fuck that! This is ours. We did this."

"I know but . . ."

"No buts. You can't kill our baby."

"I'm just not ready to be somebody's mother," she reasoned.

"You will make a perfect mother baby, besides we'll be doing it together," Antonio said. "Don't make any rash decisions. Take your time and think about it. Just do that for me."

Keisha kissed Antonio and fell asleep in his arms.

27

Hard Knock Life

"I HAVEN'T HEARD from you since I got back from North Carolina," Corey said over the phone.

"Been kind of busy."

"Too busy for me?"

Marcus was silent.

"You there?" Corey asked.

"Look, I gotta go," Marcus said hanging up the phone.

Corey just looked at his cell phone which now had a dial tone.

"Fuck it!" he said to himself.

He walked in the closet and grabbed a white Ralph Lauren polo, a pair of True Religions, and a blue Yankees fitted.

"Where is Antonio?" Corey asked Rell once he got up on the block.

"He had to take Keisha to the doctor."

"For what?" Corey asked.

"You know she pregnant nigga?"

"Nah, I didn't know," Corey said. "Damn, the nigga Antonio about to be a daddy and shit."

"Yes sir," Rell said. "Here come yo girl Toot."

"What ya'll doing?"

"Bitch, what you think we doing?" Rell said.

"Don't be ugly *boy*," she said.

"Wassup Toot?" Corey laughed.

"I just wanted to tell ya'll something."

"What?" Rell asked uninterested.

"I was over in the alley . . ." she started.

"You can stop there," Rell said. "I don't wanna hear that shit."

"Anyway *boy*. I was you know . . ."

"Sucking dick," Rell finished.

Toot rolled her eyes.

"Anyway, I heard gunshots and ran out to see what was going on and saw a silver truck drive off."

"What the fuck does that have to do with us?" Rell asked with short patience.

"That's the night yo' boy mama's house got shot up."

"What kind of truck was it?" he asked.

"One of them fancy, expensive kind," she said.

Rell put something in her hand and she scurried across the street where she had appeared from.

Corey was quiet.

28

Ambitionz Az A Ridah

"I SEE YOU caused quite a buzz on the street," Jermaine said. "That was the plan," Marcus responded. "I think its time for Phase II now though."

"Don't move too quickly grasshopper."

"I know what I'm doing."

"I'm just saying – pace yourself."

"I got it under control."

"Make sure that you do," Jermaine said. "I'm not dealing with any fuck up's."

"I'm getting ready to leave," Fatima said walking through the living room with denim Cavalli shorts, a pink bebe tank, and Stuart Weitzman jelly flip flops.

"Where are you going dressed like that?" Jermaine asked.

"To get my hair braided."

"Where?"

"Some chick in southeast that I keep hearing about," Fatima said. "I've actually seen some of her work and she's good."

"Do you have money?"

"Yeah, I have it. It'll be late when I get back though."

"Why is that?'

"The type of braids that I'm getting take several hours baby."

"Alright, see you when you get back."

"I want to take the truck," Fatima said doubling back.

"Get the keys from Marcus."

Marcus handed the keys to Fatima as she walked out the condo. His eyes followed her.

"Marcus," Jermaine called out to him.

"That's not you. Focus!"

"My bad."

"Don't disrespect me like that again."

"I just . . ."

"No need for apologies," Jermaine said lighting a cigarillo. "Back to this second phase of yours."

"Yeah, I think it's time."

"Well, move forward with implementing it if you think it's not too soon."

"I'm gon' need something else to push since Fatima has the Range."

"Drive yo' own shit nigga," Jermaine said watching a *Chappelle Show* DVD on that huge plasma.

"I thought I could get the Audi S8."

"Nigga, you thought wrong. You can get your SmartTrip out that expensive Dunhill wallet you got," Jermaine said stamping the cigar out. "Get the fuck out my house."

29

Good Woman Down

"I GUESS YOU keeping the baby?" Calandra asked.

"I still haven't fully made up my mind," Keisha said.

"She's keeping it," Antonio said. "Baby, I'm about to go hang out."

"Okay," she said.

Antonio kissed her stomach and then kissed her lips before he left the apartment.

"What's with Antonio being so nice?" Calandra asked.

"I know girl," Keisha laughed. "I'm trippin."

"What you doing today?"

"I'm going with Fay to a nutritionist later," Keisha said. "You?"

"I got a client in about an hour."

"Who? Bitch, you know you charge too much," Keisha joked. "Hoes in the street say you do good work but that they can't afford you."

"That's on them broke bitches. You have to pay for quality," Calandra said. "I don't really know the chick that's coming. I just know her from uptown."

"Oh, okay."

"Call me when you and Fatty . . . I mean Fay get back."

"I will," Keisha said walking Calandra to the door, giving her a nasty look.

Calandra made it home just in time. Fatima knocked on Calandra's door exactly 10 minutes before her scheduled appointment.

"Hey, how you doing?" Calandra said. "Come on in."

"I'm Fatima," she said extending her hand and looking around the apartment.

"Come on back," Calandra said walking ahead of Fatima. "You can have a seat while I finish getting everything set up."

Calandra put a few dishes in the sink, turned the oven on, and pulled her Marcel's from under the sink and sat them on the counter.

"Okay girl, I'm ready," Calandra said walking back into the living room.

"Is that your son in the pictures?" Fatima asked.

"Yeah, it is."

"How old is he?"

"He's seven."

"He's a handsome little guy."

"Thank you. Do you have any?"

"Girl *no*," Fatima stressed the no. The burden of admittance was obviously even too much for the fashionista.

The kitchen table was cluttered with drinking glasses, a chicken box, disposable plates, combs, hair clips, human and synthetic hair, beeswax and gel. Fatima pulled #2 human hair that was blended with #30 from her cognac Gucci Hobo bag.

From start to finish, it took Calandra 8 ½ hours to braid Fatima's hair. They conversed maybe 45 minutes of that off and on. Calandra took her to the bathroom and handed her a mirror so that she could see the front and the back. Fatima smiled as she ran her manicured fingers over her hidden braids.

"I like it girl," she said.

"I'm glad you do."

"You should think about opening a shop," Fatima said.

"I have. I just don't have the money to get it up and running right now. Maybe one day."

"You never know. There are always people out here with more money than they know what to do with."

"True."

They walked back in the living room and Fatima grabbed her Gucci bag and *O, At Home* magazine from the couch. She pulled a stack of $100 dollar bills from her shorts and put 10 of them in Calandra's hand.

"It's only $700," Calandra said attempting to hand her 3 bills back.

"That's for you girl. Buy that handsome little boy some Jordan's or something with it."

"Thank you . . ."

"Fatima."

"That's right. Forgive me, I'm horrible with names."

"That's fine. You'll learn it because I'll definitely be back."

"Alright girl. I appreciate you.

Corey, Rell, and Antonio were standing on the block when they spotted the silver Range Rover inching up the street. Rell and Corey reached in their waists. Gunshots rang out. The block cleared. The Rover swerved and ran up on the sidewalk. The side of it was riddled with bullet holes.

30

Change Your World

FAY STOPPED BY Keisha's after church. Calandra kept talking when she walked in the house.

"Girl, that's crazy. I had just finished braiding her damn hair," she said. "She was pretty cool; uppity but cool."

"Did they say who did it?" Keisha asked.

"Ain't nobody talking. You know the codes of the street."

"I know girl."

"Who are you talking about?" Fay asked.

"The girl who got shot driving the Range Rover last night," Keisha said.

"I hadn't heard about it," Fay said.

"I don't know how you escaped it. Everybody talking about it," Calandra said.

"Well, some of us chase drama," Fay said.

"And some of us are drama," Calandra fired back.

"And they all said Amen," Keisha joked trying to soften the tension.

"Both of you should have been with me at church this morning anyway instead of sitting around here gossiping," Fay said.

"And what do you think them old ladies doing over there in that corner?" Keisha asked.

"Gossiping," Calandra answered.

"Well, I can't speak to what they do. I can only be accountable for Fay."

"Catch us next week," Keisha said.

"Catch *her* next week," Calandra said. "I can sit at home and watch T. D. Jakes."

"I have to be in fellowship. It's too much going on out here," Fay said. "I'm actually thinking about moving."

"Moving where?" Keisha asked.

"Down south somewhere like North Carolina where Calandra people live."

"That's a big change girl," Keisha said.

"I know but it's getting too dangerous up here. I said was going to talk to Corey about selling the house," Fay said. "How is the girl who got shot?"

"Word on the street is that she's in critical condition," Calandra said.

Fay shook her head.

"Well, I was just stopping by. I'm going home to cook and get out of these clothes," Fay said.

Keisha and Calandra looked at each other.

"I'm baking some chicken," Fay said quickly.

"And what else?" Calandra asked.

"Probably some peas and a salad on the side."

"As long as its healthy," Keisha said. "We just left the nutritionist the other day."

"You two better be glad I just left church or I would be calling you out your names for trying to come for me," Fay said leaving.

"Hallelujah!" Calandra joked.

"Girl, you gon get enough," Keisha said. "How you and Rell doing?"

"I honestly think its over."

"Calandra, stop playing."

"I'm serious. It was over before it was over."

"Why you say that?"

"I just got a feeling plus Rell ain't gon do right."

"When did you figure that out?" Keisha asked.

"Everybody knew that but me – until now."

"Better late than never."

"The last time we had sex – he fucked me like it was the last time," Calandra said.

"When was that?"

"The other night. I could feel his dick in the bottom of my stomach."

"That don't sound like break-up sex. That sounds like break yo' back sex," Keisha joked.

"But there was no passion, no love. It's like I was a chick he had just met – a jump-off or some shit."

"Have you talked to him since then?"

"Not really. He said he was gon chill at his Mama house and help out over there but I know what time it is."

"I hate to hear that girl but sometimes change is good."

"But what if you not ready for the change?"

31

On My Block

MARCUS AND JERMAINE sat in the hospital room at George Washington with Fatima. They had been there for three days. Her condition was critical.

"You can go home man," Jermaine told Marcus.

"I can stay if you need me."

"Nah, go ahead. I'm good."

Fatima's hair was still as flawless as when she left Calandra's. An IV needle was pumping into her arm. She was asleep. Her family was on their way from New York.

Marcus hopped on the Metro at Foggy Bottom-GWU and was looking right in Corey's face. He walked past him and said nothing.

"Back on the train?" Corey asked.

Marcus ignored him.

"It's like that nigga?"

"Keep your voice down," Marcus commanded.

"I thought that was your Range?"

"You jumping to conclusions slim," Marcus said.

"I don't think so. I know exactly what the fuck is going on and you best believe that your boss' girl ain't the last victim," Corey said getting off at Shaw-Howard U.

Corey walked down Georgia Avenue to Best Cuts. It was Thursday and the shop was pretty quiet. Corey was in the chair waiting on his Jamaican barber to come from the back. *106 & Park* was playing on the front television.

"What happened to the girl with the phat ass who used to be on here," a dude with dreadlocks asked out the blue.

"You must be talking about Free?" the middle barber responded.

"Yeah, that's her."

"They fired her ass a long time ago. Where the fuck you been?" a stocky guy with a mole on his face, commented.

"Nigga, no they didn't. She quit so she could work on her album," a barber at the front of the shop said.

"What damn album?" the dreaded dude asked. "Is it out? I take it you have it since you know so damn much."

"Not yet," the barber at the front said. "She may have gotten dropped by her label by now."

"Like I said, she got fired," the dude with the mole said.

"Her ass still fat though," everyone agreed, laughing.

A young dude rocking Black Label and Nike boots walked in the shop. The pendant around his neck said LIL MAN. He milled around a lil bit before he started talking shit.

"They say its gon be blood in the streets until my dude find out who shot up his truck and put his girl in the hospital," the youngster said.

"Everybody been talking about that," the owner of the shop chimed in.

"It's about to get real out here in these streets, no bullshit!" the kid went on.

Corey's barber brushed his hair down and picked up the clippers. The entire shop was listening to the young dude recount what Corey was already privy to. The details of the shooting spewed from the young dude's mouth.

"You know a lot about it son. Were you there?" the owner asked.

The young dude ignored the question and kept talking. He would occasionally look in Corey's direction and smirk. Corey was uneasy but didn't want to make any moves in the shop.

Everybody started commenting on the shooting.

"I heard that nigga Jermaine don't fuck around," the dreadhead said.

"You know they say he got the whole 3rd District on payroll," an older man commented.

"That nigga ain't shit," a young dope boy said looking through a *Vibe* magazine.

"I bet you won't say that shit to him," the dreadlocked dude said.

"I'll say it to him *and* fuck that fine ass girl of his once she gets healed," the dope boy said.

"You better pipe down yungin," the owner said. "Before we be reading about yo lil young ass in the *Post*."

"Whatever," the kid said.

"You better listen to homeboy," the youngster wearing the Black Label and Nike boots said to the dope boy as he left out the shop.

32

Burn

"I THINK THAT nigga Corey sleeping with the enemy," Rell said to Antonio.

"What the fuck you talking about?" Antonio asked. "Don't involve me in that pseudo-relationship shit you two got going on."

"Nigga, I'm serious. I'm hearing that Corey been seen jumping out of that silver truck we shot up."

"That can't be. Why hasn't he said anything?"

"Good question."

"That's not like him to hold back on us like that. There has to be more to it. I mean, my mother's house got shot up and she could have been inside it," Antonio said. "I know he not letting dick cloud his judgment."

"You just never know," Rell said.

"Fuck that! Corey is my homeboy. He wouldn't sell me out like that."

"I told that nigga in Charlotte that he was talking too much."

"Yeah, we all make mistakes though."

"But that mistake could have cost your mom her life. And your mom is like a mom to me. You know that."

"Where Corey at anyway?"

"It's Thursday so he probably at the barbershop."

Rell's phone rang for the third time. And for the third time, he ignored it.

"Who the fuck blowing you up?"

"Calandra crazy ass," Rell said.

"Answer it and talk to her."

"And tell her what?"

"That you decided to move on."

"She knows."

"How the fuck she know if you didn't tell her."

"Bitches can sense shit like that," Rell said laughing.

"Nah, you being the bitch for not being a man," Antonio said flipping the TV to *Jeopardy!*

33

Got 'Til It's Gone

COREY DROPPED $30 in his barber's hand and left the shop giving dap to a few of the dudes he passed. It was hot as hell and Corey was sweating. He stopped by Labamba's where you can catch some Howard honey's having lunch but since school was out for the summer, the hang out spot was kind of empty.

Corey ordered a chicken sandwich with lettuce and tomato; fries with salt, pepper, and ketchup; and iced tea. He added three chocolate chip cookies when his order was ready. On his way out, he bumped into the lil dude who was making noise about the Range Rover shooting in the barbershop.

"Watch yourself partner," the youngin said who was now with a group of dudes.

"Fuck you son," Corey said.

"You got a lot of mouth for a nigga who is uncertain of his future."

"What the fuck you talking about moe?"

"Exactly. Ain't you a southeast nigga? What the fuck you doing up here?" the young boy said. "They ain't got no shops in the hood?"

"You talk real greasy for a lil nigga," Corey said.

"And you try to be real gangsta for a nigga who suck dick."

Corey dropped his food and stole on the youngster. Realizing that he was out-numbered, he jumped on the number 70 bus right outside Labamba's. Corey pulled out his phone and called Rell whose phone automatically went to voicemail.

"Yo son, tell Antonio that Alex Trebek just retired," he said into the phone.

That was their code for 'the streets are hot and it's time to lay low or maybe even leave town.'

Corey stayed on the bus instead of getting off and taking the train. He put his earpiece in and cued up his iPod. The bus finally made it to Corey's stop. He jumped off and began the short walk to his house. His phone was ringing but he couldn't hear it because "It Was A Good Day" by Ice Cube was seeping through his ears via the iPod. Corey was a huge Cube fan from his N.W.A. days. He checked the mailbox and walked up to the front door.

One, two, three and eventually six bullets went through Corey's body as he put his key in the door. A burgundy 1997 Chevy Lumina with dark windows and drive out tags squealed off. Toot ran over to the house and bent over Corey's body as he took his last breath. Her eyes welled with tears as she screamed out for help.

Fay pulled up and got out of the truck, leaving the engine running. Corey's lifeless body lay there in a pool of his own blood. Fay wailed as she dropped to her knees. Corey's phone started ringing again. Toot picked it up and answered it.

"Hello," she said solemnly.

"Who the fuck is this?" Rell's voice commanded knowing that the voice on the other end of the phone wasn't Corey's.

"You should get over here."

"Over where?" he asked.

"Corey and Fay's," Toot said hanging up.

The ambulance arrived before Rell did. A medic pulled a white sheet over Corey's entire body after they put him on a stretcher. Antonio and Rell found Fay still on her knees on the porch, crying and praying. Toot was trying to comfort her through her own tears. Rell took off, pushing past emergency personnel, and jumped into the back of the ambulance.

He pulled the white cover from over Corey's bullet-riddled body. He threw up immediately. Antonio helped the ER staff to get Rell out of the ambulance. Rell was screaming and crying and swearing revenge on Corey's killer. Fay had passed out and a new medical team was bringing her to. The hood stopped as sirens blared and blood dripped.

34

Cry On

Precious Lord, take my hand,
Lead me on, let me stand,
I am tired, I am weak, I am worn;
Through the storm, through the night,
Lead me on to the light

Take my hand, precious Lord,
Lead me home.

FAY HAD TO stop twice to compose herself as she sang "Precious Lord" in a capacity-filled church. On the same pew as Fay's mom and Corey's mother; were Keisha, Calandra, Antonio, and Rell. Calandra held Keisha's hand tightly as Keisha cried on Antonio's shoulder.

Two ushers had to take Rell out of the sanctuary. Antonio stood and talked about how much he admired Corey for always being true to who he was. He reminisced about growing up with Corey and watching him become a man, a friend, a brother. Tears rolled down his face as he recounted anecdotes about his partner. Keisha and Calandra followed with moving accounts of Corey's personality. Fay and Rell, although they attempted, were unable to finish their tributes.

Corey's mother stood and wiped tears from her eyes.

"Corey and I didn't always see eye to eye. He marched to the beat of a drum I wasn't prepared to hear played. But he was my son. My baby boy. And I loved him. I always will."

She sat down and bowed her head as Fay's mother comforted her. They all went around and viewed the body. Corey looked the same as he always did – rubber band complexion, dusty curls, and butterscotch eyes. He looked like he was asleep. Peaceful, even.

Antonio and Rell along with several of the deacons in the church served as pallbearers and took the casket out of the church after the viewing. The procession to the interment in the limousine was ghastly. No one spoke. There was silent weeping and a box of Kleenex being passed.

Everyone was still trying to come to terms with what had happened. No one had made any headway toward a resolution. The minister rambled on about being called home, resting places, and other by-the-book mantras commonly quoted at burials. His words comforted no one. The shock and pain were too new. Too deep.

Corey had not only marched to the beat of his own drum, but he played and choreographed the whole ordeal. The void he left would probably never be filled as his friends and family continued through life with only his memories, an obituary, and each other.

35

No More Drama

I T WAS HUMID as hell the last Saturday morning of August. Calandra and Keisha were helping Fay pack up the last of her things. The mood in the house that Fay and Corey had grown up in was nostalgic but not somber. The most difficult chore was boxing the belongings of Corey.

There were tons of orange and tan Nike shoe boxes, clothes were scattered around the room in disarray, pictures of and with family members were stuck to the mirror with tape, a framed picture of Corey, Antonio, and Rell sat on his nightstand. Condoms were under the bed, DVD's, video games, and a diary of escapades littered the room. The sun shone brightly through the window.

Corey's room was a testament of his life – a suave cat with love for family and friends and an appetite for sex and fun. All three women laughed, cried, and taped boxes as they reminisced.

Fay locked the door to her grandmother's house for the last time, rubbing her thumb across a dried splatter of blood in the door jamb. She passed the FOR SALE sign in the yard as Keisha and Calandra waited by her truck. Fay was headed to North Carolina.

She hugged Keisha.

"You better visit bitch," Fay said.

"Let me find out you cursing," Keisha joked.

"God is *working* on me but he hasn't totally *worked* it out," Fay said. "I'm a work in progress."

"You know we'll be down there," Keisha said.

"I know we haven't always clicked but I appreciate you asking your parents if I could stay with them until I get on my feet down there."

"Fay, I couldn't see it going down any other way. My parents have plenty of space plus my mom enjoyed your company. They're glad to help you," Calandra said.

"I'm just sayin . . . you didn't have to do that."

"I owe you that much," Calandra said. "Go down there and enjoy the relative peace that Charlotte can offer."

"I plan to," Fay said hugging Calandra.

"And don't go down there letting Mrs. Katharine reverse all that hard work you've put in by eating all that good home-cooked food," Keisha said.

"Girl, that's gon be the hardest part," Fay laughed. "You know how Mrs. Katharine throws down but I'm loving that I've lost 15 pounds so I'm gonna try to stay focused."

"You better," Keisha and Calandra said.

They watched as Fay got in the truck and pulled off.

"I love her fat ass," Calandra joked.

"So it took her leaving for you to realize that?"

"Better late than never," Calandra asked.

"Anyway, when does Lil' Tony and Jeremy get back?" Keisha asked as she and Calandra got in Antonio's Chrysler 300.

"They left about an hour ago so I expect they'll be here sometime early evening."

"Are they coming back on the bus?"

"Nah, Jeremy's mother went up there to get them," Calandra said.

"School starts next week doesn't it?"

"Yeah, I can't believe the summer is gone girl."

"I know, me either," Keisha said.

"It's been one wild as summer though."

"Bitch, yo' winters are wild too," Keisha joked.

"Fuck you!"

"Speaking of fucked up – did you hear about the dude Corey was messing around with?" Keisha asked.

"Nah, what happened?"

"They found that dude along with the burgundy Lumina he was driving floating in the Anacostia River."

"Damn, that's fucked up," Calandra said. "Serves his bitch ass right."

"Aren't you the same chick who wanted to fight Corey over the Rell rumors?"

"Keisha, you know like I know that those weren't rumors. It was what it was. I'm like the chicks Corey talked about who do what they were going to already do anyway."

"That's big of you to say. Bitch, you got a fever? First you hollering you love Fay and now admitting that you knew yo man was fucking around with his boy."

"You can't live in the drama forever Keisha."

"Speaking of – did you ever hear anymore about that chick whose hair you braided?"

"Last I heard, she and ole boy moved to New Jersey somewhere."

"How is she though? She was in the hospital for about a week or so, wasn't she?"

"Longer than that but I think she's cool now. Or as cool as she can be considering what happened to her," Calandra said. "Several of the bullets barely missed her vital organs."

"That's fucked up," Keisha said.

"It sure is especially since she was about to become a regular client at $700 a pop."

"I see you won't ever change."

"For what?" Calandra asked. "I gotta pay Antonio back for frontin' me the loot to open the shop."

"Girl, Antonio isn't in any hurry for that money."

"Well, I don't like owing people."

The Chrysler 300 pulled up in front of Forever Braids, Calandra's braid and style shop.

"What date did you decide for the grand opening?" Keisha asked.

"A week from today."

"You nervous?"

"Hell nah, I'm excited as shit."

"I wish I could say that," Keisha said.

"Why? What's wrong?"

"I'm so damn nervous about this baby, its not funny."

"You'll be fine plus you have plenty of help."

Calandra grabbed a new box of Marcels from the trunk of the car and she and Keisha walked into the shop where a crew of six were busy putting the finishing touches on the shop. Rell and Antonio were in the back office smoking. *Jeopardy!* was playing on a plasma screen suspended from the ceiling.

"Don't be smoking in my damn shop," Calandra said. " . . . when I'm not here now pass the blunt."

They all laughed.

"Baby, I think you should go up front while we finish this," Antonio said to Keisha. "I don't want this second hand smoke fucking with you or the baby."

"Let me holla at you for a minute," Rell said grabbing Calandra by the arm.

"What is it?" she asked.

"Yo, I just wanted to apologize for the way things ended," he said.

"It's cool," she said.

"No, it's not. I should have been man enough to say that the relationship between us had ran past its expiration date."

"You don't owe me anything Rell," Calandra said. "I enjoyed every minute of you when I had you. But, now that's over. I'm a big girl. I'll be fine."

"I know ma," he said reaching out and hugging Calandra.

"We're about to leave," Keisha said walking to the back supply room where Rell and Calandra were.

"Alright girl. I'll call you later."

Calandra and Rell continued to organize her shop while the expecting parents headed home.

Antonio and Keisha laid in bed thinking about baby names. One after one, names were shot down. Keisha closed her eyes as Antonio rubbed her protruding stomach.

"I think his name should be Corey," she said.

Antonio froze, flooded with memories of his boy.

"I think that's perfect baby," Antonio said. "I knew there was a reason that you were supposed to keep this baby. My mama always said that God never takes a life without giving life."

Antonio kissed Keisha's forehead and turned out the light beside the bed.

Just outside the apartment, parked approximately where the silver Range Rover had been parking, was a Black Charger idling. The head lights came on. The car sped off. The personalized license plates read: LIL MAN.

An excerpt from the novel that took me five years to write
and one extensive year of research – My masterpiece:

Three Sisters